High Fyelds

THE BLACK STALLION

MAE MCKINNON

DRAGONQUILL PUBLISHING

Also by Mae McKinnon

DAWN OF THE WINDS
(credited as M. Aei)

WOLF'S BANE
(credited as M. Aei)

ACADEMIA DRACONIA

THE DAMSEL AND THE DRAGON

MAGICAL MISCHIEF – A MOTIONBOOK

HIGH FYELDS – A NEW BEGINNING

HIGH FYELDS – THE BIG RACE

YOU'RE A DRAGON – A GAMEBOOK

THE SOUL WITHIN

SILBERWING

LORD OF THE WIND

MOONTOUCHED

ISLAND OF ILLUSION

HIGH FYELDS – THE BLACK STALLION

TOGETHER WITH
A.R.Lachance. Elizabeth-Rose Best. Ian Gough & Kris Hawley.

FANTASY UNBOUND – AN ANTHOLOGY

High Fyelds

THE BLACK STALLION

HIGH FYELDS: THE BLACK STALLION
A DragonQuill book

SOS Logo designed by Nightpark
Gothic Extras B by Dharma type
Interior & Cover Design by Marlene Ockersse
Riky Vampdator font by Riky Vampdator
Black Chancery font by Doug

First Printed in 2024

ISBN: 978-9918-9562-4-1
A CIP catalogue record for this book is available from the National Library of Malta

DragonQuill Publishing
www.dragonsandquill.com

"We ask before we bite"

A.A.

CONTENTS

GOOD MORNING?

Sam watched the antics of Harlan Illusion as the slender stallion excitedly bounced between the middle of the yard and the road that led out beyond the stables. Each time he raced down the road only to screech to a halt, dig his hooves into the ground, throw himself around, and trot back to the yard head held high and proud, mane and tail streaming behind him.

He looked very pleased with himself, Sam thought. Though, if running had been all the trias had been doing, Sam would have been a lot happier.

Keeping his distance, not wanting an errant flying hoof to his head*, the tall, slender, Seranthiem said out loud what he'd until now had kept to himself.

'Are you absolutely *certain* Harlan's not actually a dog that was accidentally transformed into the shape of a horse?' he asked.

Rather than getting offended, Erina merely let out the closest thing he'd ever heard to a "guffaw". Turning her attention away from the red, black, and white horse she threw some of the empty grain sacks over her shoulder.

'Sam. Dear Sam. This is Darklight Valley. I'm not *sure* about *anything*!'

Tugging at the end of his ponytail, Seranthiem stifled a sigh. She had him there. This *was* Darklight Valley. The place was as unpredictable as the deep ocean and, occasionally, just as volatile.

Much like the weather this time of the year it seemed. Spring had arrived,

* Or anywhere else on his body for that matter.

bringing with it both warmer weather as well as the promise of five seasons every hour, on the hour.

It had also brought him. Well, technically speaking Seranthiem had brought himself, but the new employment contract he'd signed a few months back might have had something to do with the why.

The how was a very different question. Sam still wasn't entirely clear on that part. Wave Rock, his trusty dun, had carried him here, yes. But entering the Valley had hardly been straight forward. In fact, thinking back on it, it was difficult to define when exactly they'd stopped being where they'd been and had come to be where they were.

Normally, Sam's was proud of his memory. It served him well.

Of course "normal" was perhaps not the word he'd attribute to anything that had happened to him since that day. When he'd first heard of Darklight Valley, back at Epsilon Court, going there had promised to be a welcome break to the monotony of, well, everything.

Currently his life was anything *but* monotonous. It seemed the Universe had a sense of humour and had decided to make up for all those years of very little excitement all at once.

At least, some days that's certainly what it felt like. And it hadn't even been a month since he'd arrived.

Though *that* might have a little something to do with that Darklight Valley was actually a mesa of sorts. It certainly wasn't the word he'd chose to describe a towering slab of rock reaching so far up into the atmosphere that, by any scientific measurement, rhyme, or reason, nothing up here should have been able to breathe. Partly because of the lack of oxygen, but also because anyone roaming about at these heights should have been frozen solid*.

This didn't stop Sam from being here, obviously. And, judging by what he'd seen over the last couple of weeks since he'd arrived, it clearly hadn't stopped anyone else in the Valley, either. If anything, the wildlife here positively thrived. It was so natural it had to be, he thought, *unnatural*. Though the *how* for that continued to remain as elusive as the first one.

One thing was certain: his new employer fitted right in, contradictions and all. He didn't feel he did. Not yet.

* Ergo, therefore not moving about at all.

Maybe that would come. He'd have to get used to this strange land first. As he continued walking through the yard of the small stable*, Sam let the tiniest frown caress his brow. Currently, the afternoon breeze was filled with the scent of warm grass with a heavy side-note of horse.

While it felt pleasant on his soft skin, he forced himself to contain the grumbles as, for the umpteenth time since this morning, he tucked a few strands of long silver hair behind an ear. Every morning he put his hair up in a simple, serviceable, high ponytail. Every day, it strained, one strand at a time, to escape it.

He didn't have to walk far to get from one end of the stable to the other, so you'd think the wind had less opportunity to mess around. But he spent far more time outdoors than in the house and far more time working than preening — not that anyone would have guessed by looking at him.

The main house, a sturdy construction made largely from grey rocks and plaster, as well as most of the outbuildings, including the actual stables, were nestled among green, verdant, fields. Here and there trees, alone or in small clusters, dotted the immediate area leading up to leafy, airy, woods that brought welcome shade during the middle of the day.

It was the sort of picture postcard where you expected to hear an eagle, or a hawk, cry out above you as you looked up. Idyllic, that was the word he was looking for.

He really hoped that this new employer of his, Erina Darklight, had been joking when she'd warned him about him possibly getting eaten if he strayed too far from the main compound.

It might have been a joke, but, just in case it wasn't, Sam had kept his guard up when out and about. There was a great deal of that here. In fact, the entire Valley mostly consisted of *out and about*. From the rolling hills to ancient forests and mountains that reached the sky.

The stables were, in comparison, minuscule. Actually, looking around, it had to be the smallest place he'd ever worked at.

Sam wasn't going to let that little fact fool him. There was a reason he'd accepted this job. There were a lot of rumours about High Fyelds and if even

* Small in comparison to what he was used to, that was. What High Fyelds lacked in buildings it made up for in … eh, everything else?

a third of those were halfway true… Well, how could he say no?

How did the old saying go? Curiosity killed the cat?

Sam felt a small smile tug at the corners of his lips. 'Good thing I'm not a cat then,' he murmured.

'Hmm, what was that?' the only other person around asked.

'Nothing, My Lady,' Sam quickly replied.

Brought out of his reverie by a small moving cloud of dust and the thunder of hooves, Seranthiem casually flowed out of the way as, again, Harlan Illusion came flying past him.

'You'd think he'd never been able to run, the way he's carrying on,' Erina said, shaking her head at the sight. 'I mean, it must have been *a whole hour* since we got back.'

Sam refrained from any direct comments. The foraging trip this morning had been, largely, successful … as long as you didn't count having disturbed a very angry red kelpie.

You'd think, spending almost all their life in water, they'd be slow on land. Not even a little. This one had weaved in and out among the trees with the grace of a trained ballet dancer, their elongated jaws snapping and clicking at their heels.

It was times like those that made Sam wonder why *anyone* would want to make a place like this into their home when they *had* the option to leave. Only for his brain to immediately remind him of that the person in question was Erina and suddenly it all made sense.

Which was impressive, because so far, that was about the only thing that did.

Maybe he was just holding on to hope that there would one day be a rational explanation for everything the same way a man drowning in a stormy sea desperately clung on to the nearest piece of flotsam? In the meantime he tried to not let the constant barrage of surprises that this place — and his new boss — threw at him, show.

Besides, who was he to judge? Erina was hardly the first person to find a refuge away from, well, everything and everyone. After all, he was here, too.

Mind you, he usually preferred his chosen sanctum to come with a few more amenities; like working electricity and hot showers. Not to mention a lot more books.

Not that you couldn't get hot water here. It was just a lot of extra work and, most of the time, not really worth it in his mind. If there was a secret to do it another way, he hadn't found it yet.

It was things like these that reminded Seranthiem of the simple, but rather important factor, that nothing — and he'd only recently started appreciating just how extensive that *nothing* really was — could enter Darklight Valley without permission*.

That was a comforting thought for someone who disliked unexpected visitors and surprises, for all that he was a lot better about dealing with either than Erina was.

He'd certainly never threatened to bite someone's head off if they showed up without an invitation. Very undignified. Also, apparently, very effective, from what he'd seen of the reactions to when Erina skipped diplomacy and went straight for the jugular when she'd had enough.

Sam suspected that this ability to flick a switch was perhaps one of the reason she'd been so highly sought after in her old job as a Cognitor. Not that he was familiar with her past beyond what little official details he'd been able to gleam from his diom before accepting this job. It wasn't like Erina ever volunteered to share.

Her past stayed just that, the past. But you were hardly successful in that line of work she'd been in by being absentminded and walking into walls a lot, which was the side of her he was more familiar with.

Now that he thought about it, it also begged the question of who — or what — was choosing who could enter and exit the Valley. *When* they could enter. Was it a person? An unknown entity? A natural phenomenon?

Judging by Erina's grumblings about it, it certainly wasn't her. Another thing which had taken Sam by surprise. He felt he was storing those up. Surprises that was. He hoped they wouldn't all burst out from behind a mental dam one day when the pressure simply became too much.

Most of the time Sam could dismiss it all to the unplumbed depths of lost thoughts. Sometimes, though, after a particularly strong surprise, it left behind an uncomfortable knot of worry gnawing on his insides.

* Or leave, which most people would find a whole lot more disconcerting.

Just what had he gotten himself into?

Well, aside from dodging overenthusiastic and excited horses gambolling around the grounds like there was no tomorrow while he was trying to work, that was.

❊❊❊

In comparison to, almost, every afternoon, mornings around the stable were quiet affairs.

'And a good morning to you, too,' Sam said as the red, white, and black, painted trias trotted over from the far end of the field, ears pricked forward, the moment he'd heard the front door to the main house open.

He reached out and rubbed the inquisitive bald face right between the eyes. Harlan nickered in turn.

'Yes, yes, I'll give you a good brushing, I promise. Later,' Sam said. 'You too, Wave,' he added as the dun nuzzled him from the side, lipping the sleeve of his shirt.

Wave Rock was always happy to see him. But the first few days after Sam had arrived, this morning routine had been one of disappointment for Harlan. It wasn't "his person" who'd miraculously awoken shortly after sunrise.

It hadn't, however, taken long before the fact that Sam waking up early also meant he got breakfast early had firmly entrenched the silver haired man as Harlan's second favourite person. Now he greeted him with almost as much enthusiasm. At least in the morning.

He would, of course, repeat the process when his *actual* person finally dragged themselves out of slumberland. There was always the possibility that the early morning zombie would run entirely on routine and then he'd have a second breakfast on his hands. Well, hooves.

And if not, he was content with making do with some treats, pets, and a promise to "head out" a bit later.

Finishing up a few more chores to the trilling morning songs of birds he didn't yet know the names of, Sam eventually glanced up at the suns and decided that enough of the day had passed already. Pulling off the thick leather gloves he'd been wearing he carefully put the iron tools back into place. Drawing some clean water from the well in the centre of the yard he had a quick wash before heading back into the main building. It was time to make an early lunch.

The horses had eaten hours ago. So had he. There was, however, one at High Fyelds for whom mornings, and even more so, breakfast, was an alien concept.

Sam rapped his knuckles lightly on the wooden door to the master bedroom. When there was no answer, he simply counted to ten, then repeated the process.

There came an incoherent set of grumbles from the other side of the thick, knotted, wood. The grunts were a direct response to the, very light, rapping but they didn't sound quite human.

'My Lady, brunch is ready,' Sam said.

There was another set of unintelligible, but louder, noises from the room beyond. Annoyed ones.

Sam sighed.

It was the same nearly every morning. Though, personally, he was loathe to even call this time of day morning. He'd already been up for many hours. Enough that he'd gotten half a day's chores done.

Sam enjoyed the early hours. Watching the sun rise, bringing light to a dark world. It always made him feel hopeful towards what the new day would bring.

Erina … did not.

As she appeared, hunched over, bleary eyed, and with her hair in that fashionable birdsnest-never-seen-a-hairbrush style, she narrowly stopped herself from walking into the hallway wall. Brown eyes barely able to focus, she shot Sam a look of absolute disgust.

'Head's rolling,' Erina mumbled.

It was never quite clear if that was meant to be a threat or merely the current state of things.

Sam wondered if she'd happily lop someone's head off for forcing her to be awake at this hour if it wasn't legally, and morally, wrong. He hoped not.

'Good Morning, My Lady,' he said placidly.

The response was far from coherent.

'I *really* wish you'd just make food for you and let me sleep,' Erina grumbled as she sat down at the stout wooden table in the kitchen.

It had been a bit of a shock the first time. Breakfast, that was. Up until that point she hadn't even known Sam could cook. It hadn't been on his resume and he'd never mentioned it at the interview.

Brunch wasn't all that high on her list of times to enjoy food, but at least it was better than breakfast. A word that should, by all rights, be excised.

Today, as had become customary, several dishes were on offer. At any other hour of the day the scents drifting up would have made her salivate. Right now she had a hard time remembering how to hold a fork.

'Not everyone is suited to live off a meal served only when they remember to eat,' Sam pointed out as he deftly shifted some of the plates around.

Or live on grilled meat. The stables grew carrots, but he was pretty sure the vegetable plot for those was mostly for Harlan's benefit.

'Not everyone can survive on the *idea* of sleep rather than sleep itself,' Erina retorted.

Sam slid one of the plates over as, eyelids drooping, the four pronged piece of cutlery in Erina's hand rebounded from the table top. She sleepily managed to stab her fork into the smoked fish on the second try.

'Horrid invention, mornings,' she grumbled.

'Duly noted, My Lady,' Sam replied. 'May I tempt you to another fried potato?'

'Mhm… maybe just one. We still need to go up the moors today. Think you're up for the ride? It's a tricky one.'

Sam gave an affirmative nod. 'Of course, My Lady,' he said. 'Shall I saddle the horses?'

Erina ignore the question or, perhaps, she had never heard it. 'That's settled then,' she said. 'Just … let me wake up first.'

That was, probably, the safer option, Sam admitted. While he trusted Wave Rock implicitly, trusting the Valley was a different thing entirely. He'd learnt that the hard way.

As it had turned out, Erina *hadn't* been joking about the warning she'd given him earlier. Sometimes, the fauna considering you a tasty snack was the least of your problems. In some places it was the *landscape* that you had to look out for. And not for such obvious reasons as loose rocks, falling trees, or walking into a bog.

As such, he'd only recently started making larger circles around the stables. The immediate surroundings didn't seem to hold anything too dangerous. Certainly no unexpected fields of live geysers or rocks that sank beneath your feet as you traversed what you'd thought was a natural bridge across a lake.

The latter *had* happened to Erina … once. One of the many examples she'd shared with him about what could go wrong if you, or, more accurately, he, strayed from the, well, not path exactly, but certainly the better known areas.

It hadn't gone unnoticed by him that this was not advice she seemed to adhere to herself.

While this place didn't seem to follow any rules Sam could pinpoint, it wasn't as if he wasn't familiar with the idea. As an entire solar system's worth of planets, this one was nice enough, but by its very nature it was hardly what you would deem safe.

The world of Casticia was one where you quickly learned to expect the unexpected from a very young age. Here, in the Valley, there was simply a lot less space between, well, everything.

Most of the time.

Since the newly minted DragonCorps had taken up surveying, it had proven without a shadow of a doubt that while the satellites did show all the planet* they didn't show *all* the planet.

Sometimes they didn't even show the same thing as another satellite. Same with the drones. What the individual dragons and riders brought back tales of were, while coming in at a slower rate, at least consistent.

Personally, Erina hadn't been the least bit surprised when this had started happening. By then she'd had plenty of experiences with places that were but wasn't.

* But not the Valley, which was still refusing to budge on that idea. Maybe it was camera shy?

WE"R"TREES

It was called High Fyelds Stables, right? For something like that, there weren't exactly a whole lot of horses — or even other animals — here. That was something that *still* surprised Sam.

Before he'd arrived, and brought Wave Rock with him, there had, in fact, been a total of *one* horse at the stable. Sam didn't count all the ones running wild in the Valley itself. And while Harlan was a nice enough horse, it was still a bit odd in his eyes.

He'd have thought that Erina would have had the sense to at least have a couple of other horses. If for no other reason than that Harlan was hardly built to handle all types of duties equally. Having a team to pull the hay wagon would have been so much easier.

But then, the entire place had also contained the entirety of *one* person. What did she do when *she* was the one that got injured?

To be honest, when High Fyelds had been described as a "small" stable, he hadn't imagined it was the actual number of box stalls they'd been talking about. Or the amount of people "working" here.

Priorities, that's what Erina called it. Sam wasn't so sure. It hadn't taken him long to realize that Erina got along far better with critters than she did with people. Which made the lack of domestic ones around even more surprising. You'd have thought she'd wanted the extra help.

If he ever needed to bring up an example of someone who wasn't a people-person in the future, Erina would be exhibit A front and centre.

A very diplomatic one — when necessary — but a non-people person nonetheless. Though he'd soon learnt to recognize the glint in her eyes that betrayed her "I would like the wring your intestines into pretzels and then pull them out of your nose" inner monologue. So far he'd only seen that expression directed at pieces of paper. Correspondence from outside the Valley picked up … actually, he didn't know how or when they were collected.

Sam sighed. The lack of "proper" communication was becoming a nuisance. He'd never thought he'd miss his diom so much.

At the moment he was leaning on a partly built fence, made out of what must have been entwined young saplings, while questioning his life's choices. Or, at least, *this* choice.

Not the one about deciding to accept this job. Nor the one about coming along — as if he'd had a choice —today, up to the "machine park" as Erina called it.

No. Sam winced. The reason was far more mundane. Moss green was simply not a good colour on Harlan. The new halter was clashing terribly with the red, white, and black of his painted coat.

But his usual one had broken and, Erina, having been in a hurry, had simply grabbed one from a barrel filled with pieces of "spare" tack. Most of it was in a state of disrepair. Hence why it had been consigned to the barrel in the tack room, he presumed.

The halter was very visible, he had to admit that. From what he'd seen around the stable so far, fashion was *not* the reason behind any choices made here. While Sam prescribed to the adage of utility as much as the next person, that wasn't the only consideration he took into account when picking one thing over the other. Especially not when it came to accessories.

Even his "hardwearing" working clothes* were chosen deliberately and carefully. He liked taking his time. He tried to put the same care and attention to everything he did.

The same could not be said about the only other person present. He glanced over to where Erina was standing. So far he hadn't seen any evidence of that she paid any attention at all — if seeing her in the same clothes three

* The "safe to throw half a bucket of paint over and not worry" kind.

days in a row was anything to judge by.

Or maybe she had picked out the best options already and now simply had ten copies of the exact same shirt and trousers? How would he tell? They all looked the same. The fact that they were all — if indeed there were a "them" — a sort of faded black didn't help.

Mismatched as they were, the two of them watched as Harlan dashed back and forth in the field they were in trying to entice Wave Rock to play with him. Even with the "contraptions" that lined the stream running through the area there was more than enough space until the trees of the forest truly began to encroach on the open territory once more.

Sam imagined that in high summer the tall grasses would make it look more like a couple of acres of farmland, golden wheat axes rippling in the wind, than the sprightly young green shoots that were currently growing almost as enthusiastically as the animals cavorting through them.

'At least they haven't run straight into the machinery,' Erina pointed out, shaking her head at the sight.

Break time over, they returned to stacking the hay wagon. Over half of the bales still sat where the machine had spat them out.

'Never considered a dog?' Sam asked, seemingly out of the blue. To him High Fyelds seemed like the kind of place that would have at least one dog, probably more. Both for companionship and protection.

'Considered, yes,' Erina replied as her fingers tried to dig into the bale she'd been trying to shift from where it had wedged itself sideways on top of another. It refused to budge.

Only being the second layer, she still had to stand on tip-toe to have any chance to move it.

'Good thing we didn't stack them any higher,' Erina gave the bale another, heavy, tug.

She gritted her teeth as Seranthiem took a couple of steps over and pushed it into place with one hand.

'Damnit, Sam. What's with this curse of being short?' Erina groused.

'I wouldn't know, My Lady,' Sam replied, keeping his face straight. 'I'm certain it's advantageous in other ways.'

'How very diplomatic of you,' Erina chuckled and shook her head. 'Was that the last one? It was, wasn't it?'

'It wasn't,' Sam said, nodding towards the stack by the wooden machine that had created them.

'Come on! There *can't* be that many left!'

But there was, much to Erina's chagrin. By the time they could step back to admire their handiwork, they were both drenched. The hay wagon did look very neatly loaded though, she had to admit.

'I can't believe I used to do all of this *on my own*,' Erina said.

'Are you certain it wouldn't be easier to have these shipped in?' Sam asked.

Erina snorted. 'Only if I want the delivery to never arrive,' she said. 'Trust me, I've tried. It'd certainly have made my life a lot easier. It's not like I've given myself back ache by choice you know.'

'I—

'It's not like I'm doing all this the hard way because I'm a sort of sado-masochist.'

Seranthiem ignored that last jab on purpose. 'At least we didn't need to tie all these by hand,' he acknowledged, nodding towards the water-powered contraption that had been built* at the nearby waterway.

This one was just a little larger than the one running across the far field outside the stable itself. Rather than bubbling happily, the rocky bottom visible from the surface, this one was a slow, but steady, power house — literally.

Erina chuckled.

'Just wait until harvest season,' she said. 'Or, even better, your first winter.'

'I shall endeavour to do so.'

'Remind me that I should take you out on a longer excursion. This is as far from the stable as you've been since you came here, isn't it?'

'I believe so, yes,' Sam replied.

Not that the "machine park" was far. Not by Valley standards. It was still within a wagon's day of travel back and forth to High Fyelds across, mostly, flat land.

* Or at least been cobbled together, which was an entirely different visual.

That meant it was, comparatively, deceptively even, normal. Even the watercourse was, here, just that … a watercourse.

Strong enough to turn the waterwheels. Deep enough that you couldn't see the bottom — though the churning of the wheels, however slow they might be, probably had something to do with that. It disturbed the river bed and water alike. But it was exactly what you expected it to be.

Which, in her mind, made it very useful and very, very boring.

She couldn't wait to see the expression on Seranthiem's face when she showed him some of the other ones. Erina snorted again. Maybe she'd actually even catch a glimpse of him having what she'd considered an expression. For all that his face did move, it might as well have been a mask. A very serene, flawless, mask that merely changed to convey whatever he chose to convey, not what he actually felt.

Erina was the first person to admit she didn't understand people. As many had found out to their detriment, in her old job, that was not the same as not being able to read them.

Compared to people, the land was a lot easier to deal with. As were the animals that inhabited it*.

Sometimes babbling brooks that you came across were simply bubbly because of the coarse, stony, bottom they were running over. Usually not. Once she'd come across one that had *actually* been bubbling. Not boiling, just bubbling, suds and all. She'd resisted the urge to stick her fingers in it to check if it was filled with natural detergent.

Sometimes they didn't stick around and, if you went back two days later, there was no trace of that there had even been a stream there in the first place. The streams around the stable at least had the curtesy of remaining just that. Stable.

By now she'd stopped questioning everything so much and simply rolled with it.

'Oh well, time to pull my head out of the clouds and focus on what I'm doing,' Erina said. 'Working up here is a good way to lose a hand, if you don't pay attention†.'

* Plants were a different matter …

† Not that she had any experience of doing that, losing any hands, that was. Experience of not paying attention, she had plenty.

Sam wondered if she was saying it for his benefit or her own. It wasn't as if he was going to volunteer sticking his fingers into any weird machinery.

Pushing the last of the hay bales into place, Erina dusted off her hands, took a deep breath, and, on the contraption behind them, pulled one prominent wooden lever all the way down, locking it into place.

Something inside the interior went "clank". The creaking of the water-wheel continued. As did the soft splash as every paddle dipped into the water. It no longer made anything happen within. The power connection had been cut.

'Phew,' she said and rubbed at the back of her aching hands. 'That's one thing down. Time to hitch up the horses and head back, I guess.'

Meanwhile, Sam, who'd been side-eying the machinery ever since they'd first arrived, now had the time to really study it.

It was a curious looking contraption made of wood and metal (or what *looked* like wood and metal, Sam was no fool). Almost twice as tall as he was, it had to be about eight or ten meters long. He would have called it oblong in shape if the surface hadn't been filled with all sorts of pistons, valves, gears, cranks and other things he had no idea what they were. Something inside went "chugga, chugga, chugga" only when you pulled a very specific lever. There were tubes *everywhere*.

A lot of the parts could move. Everything seemed connected to everything else, though how he hadn't yet worked out. Most of the noises when in use came from the internal workings, which, obviously, he couldn't see.

How wasn't it full of errant leaves and windblown debris?

It reminded him a little of an ancient steam engine halfway through being rebuilt into something else, only this one had mostly been made out of wood and was, from his understanding, hollow.

Sam commented on this out loud*. It earned him a distinctly mischievous — or devious, he couldn't always tell them apart when it came to Erina — grin.

'You like it?' Erina asked.

'I … don't know,' Sam admitted. 'It's … unusual. Did you have this made?'

* Not the part of him not being a fool, obviously.

'Yup,' Erina said. 'Well, sort of. Someone else made the blueprints. How would I haul something this heavy out here on my own?'

'And it's made of?'

'Semblance wood* all the way.'

Erina considered what she'd said for a moment and added, 'Aside from the bits that are copper. And other … stuff.'

'As versatile a substance as always, I see,' Sam nodded. 'Do we have a maker right here?' He looked about, as if he'd be able to spot one hiding among the dahlias.

Erina scoffed at the idea. 'I didn't make it,' she clarified. 'It came in a kit. Getting it here was pure murder, mind you. Don't ask! I *did* put it together. That's got to count for something.'

It probably did, Sam thought. Some of these contraptions scattered along the length of the watercourse looked quite intricate … for all that they contained not one photon of electric current.

'Let me tell you, I think those kit instructions get written by a malevolent daemon!'

Sam hid an internal smile. By now he'd become very familiar with his employer's ability — or lack thereof — to follow instructions. Any instructions. The kind meant for other people to be able to understand easily somehow stumped her especially hard.

The power-scaling system of comprehension went something along the lines of:

Understanding the cosmic secrets of the universe: *Easy.*

Seeing the dirty dishes in the sink: *Impossible.*

Well, metaphorically, anyway. Hence why he usually ended up being the one who did them. The dishes that was.

'I'm not sure I'd go that far, My Lady,' Sam said, trying to dislodge the image now stuck in his mind without laughing out loud. 'I imagine it would have taken a lot of time.'

He looked around them. There wasn't just one of the strange machines. Though not one of them looked anything alike, they were all built around the

* Semblance wood was favoured by a lot of people. Not only did you not have to go about cutting down and dragging around all those pesky trees, but you could even get it pre-shaped if you wanted to.

same general oblong shape. The main difference seemed to be their size. Though the one with what appeared to be a giant hamster-wheel sticking partway out of it did stand out.

'Nope. I would definitely go that far,' Erina said. 'But they do say Rome wasn't built in a day.' She shrugged. 'Could be worse. I could be trying to do all *this* stuff by hand.'

That was, indeed, what she'd needed to do early on. It hadn't been until she'd been able to leave the Valley for the first time that any other options had even been on the table.

The trip down memory lane was interrupted by a dull sort of echo.

Tilting her head to one side, she hoped something hadn't gotten into one of the machines. They might not have electric wires that could be chewed, but there were plenty of other things that could go wrong.

'Do you hear that?' Erina asked.

'Hear what, My Lady?' Sam wondered.

'I'll take that as no. Seems to be coming from?' Erina put her ear to the machine she'd swear she'd turned off. 'Nope. Not this one,' she said. 'Where *is* it coming from?'

'Perhaps it would help if you would describe the sound,' Sam suggested. Scanning the area around them, every single sound, from the low droning of the insects to the neighs coming from the frolicking horses, he could identify.

'There's nothing there, My Lady,' Sam said.

'That doesn't help,' Erina muttered. She sucked in her breath, as if that somehow made her hearing better. Nothing. 'Nevermind, it's gone now.'

'It does not appear the horses were concerned,' Sam pointed out.

'That's good, at least,' Erina said. It had been an odd sound. Glancing up at the almost clear sky, she dismissed the idea that it might have come from above. Maybe it had just been her ears ringing? That happened sometimes.

Erina shrugged. 'Oh well.'

'Perhaps it was the wind?' Sam suggested. 'Or, perhaps, one of those?' He pointed towards the contraptions lined up against the banks of the small river. Powered by several waterwheels — one each — the wooden paddles splashed. The axels creaked. They turned slowly, almost lazily, but of everything out here they definitely made the most consistent noise.

There must be some sort of force multiplier inside the machines themselves, Sam figured. There was no way a single, slow, wheel on its own was enough.

'It'd provide more power if the water was faster,' Sam said as he noticed that there was a more rapid flow elsewhere on the river.

It would be so much easier if it had a name, Sam thought. He'd asked, but it seemed like for most things Erina figured that if she knew where things were that was the part that matter.

Which was fine while she had been alone, in Sam's mind. Maybe he could convince her they should name more locations? At least he could be certain the ones that *did* have names were fairly significant.

Erina shrugged. 'Sure. I *could* relocate all of this,' she said. 'Then I'd only have to deal with an even longer trudge to get there ... and going bananas trying to assemble these things again.'

Seranthiem blinked at her, realizing he'd lost track of where the conversation had been going while thinking of other things.

'Sam? Seriously? You think any of them would still be working if I did that? Recall the old trope about how you'd take apart a QDE engine and somehow always end up with more parts than you started with?'

Her companion let out a small, discreet, cough. That was, indeed, what they said. He'd never tried doing it himself. Quasi Dimensional Engineering wasn't his field of expertise.

It wasn't most other people's either...

'Now, the size of these knobs indicates the current amount of force you have to work with,' Erina patted something that looked like an abacus, only they'd misunderstood how to use it, made it round and then installed it sideways. She launching into an explanation of what did what.

Against all his effort to do otherwise, Sam felt his focus slip. It was brought back, abruptly, as his brain overheard something that his ears hadn't.

'Rabbits, My Lady?' Sam asked, confusion evident on his face.

'Yes,' Erina nodded. 'As I said, this lever here will turn anything you put into it into bales. Hay. Hats. Rabbits.'

Sam who shuddered. That sounded messy. A fact confirmed a second later.

'It's a pain to clean,' Erina told him, 'so I suggest sticking with things that are *meant* to be in bales. Or, at least, compacted.'

'Could you make food with it?'

'Technically. Not been much need when there's just been me. Suppose we could set aside one of the smaller ones, if you think that'd be useful. In the meantime, why don't you help me out with catching our four-legged goofballs so we can get this load back to the stable?'

'Of course, My Lady.' Sam made a small bow.

❉❉❉

As the weeks passed on by, spring slowly morphed into something that could be mistaken for summer, if it wasn't for the cold draft sneaking down from the mountains in the morning.

The world had woken up but it'd be a while before it started to bake … if it ever did. Seranthiem couldn't recall getting a detailed breakdown on the seasons and what they meant here. They could be confusing enough throughout the rest of the planet.

One thing he did know (it would have been impossible not to, the peak could be seen even from the very middle of the valley) was that in some of the mountains that surrounded the central core of Darklight Valley, the warmth of summer was a long way away.

Sam shaded his eyes as he tried to focus on the almost triangular, white, shape on the horizon. 'Almost summer and Snowfell still stands as a towering testament to winter eternal,' he said.

'The land of ice and snow,' Erina nodded.

Pulling her head out of the broken cabinet she'd been rummaging through for the last five minutes, she gave it a small kick. She'd gone through it two times already and not found what she was looking for despite being absolutely certain that it was there.

The corner cabinet had been dragged out into the yard some time ago. Long enough that patches of green had started to appear on the surface. It should have been empty, but, as Erina had discovered after knocking into it while walking past, something was rattling around inside.

It hadn't bothered her before, when she hadn't known. Now she couldn't get it out of her head.

'I … just … can't seem … to find it,' she growled, poking angrily at the two part opening. Straightening up, she massaged her back. 'Hope you're not planning on going there,' Erina said, throwing Sam a suspicious glance. Why else would he have brought it up?

'Wouldn't dream of it, My Lady,' Seranthiem assured her.

Not that Erina believed him. You didn't look *that* innocent if you weren't already plotting something.

'Oh? Really?' she drawled. 'Pretty sure I told you to stay away from that place, it's treacherous.'

'So I heard.'

'Let's finish up here quickly,' Erina said. 'I'm getting tired and we've got a long day ahead of us tomorrow. Let's chop this thing up. I don't think we're going to get the smell out and I'm not putting it back into the house. Whatever's hiding in it be damned.'

They never did find whatever secrets the cabinet had been holding, if any. They did, however, on the morrow, find themselves back in the saddle and well away from the stable itself.

Depending on which direction you left High Fyelds in, you could still see the buildings for quite some distance. With their current path, they'd long since lost sight of them.

The river fields of power, as Sam thought of them, did have a sort of semi visible road track where the wagon wheels had carved out a route, leading up to them.

Everywhere else, you were … just supposed to know where you were going? A map would have helped, but he wasn't sure if there even was one. Considering Erina's tendency not to name things (except in her head) he supposed that writing them down with handy, elegant, little ink drawings was too much to ask.

At the moment he just sort of let his mount lead the way, which he did by loyally following his new friend.

Harlan and Wave Rock were ambling along leisurely beside each other. It had taken far less time for the two horses to get used to working together than it had their riders*.

Right now they were picking their own way up a low hill. Only occasionally did a slight touch of a rein redirect Harlan to keep him on track of where they were heading.

As usual, none of the two-legs had shared their plans with either of them. This was okay. They'd find out when they got there. Hopefully it was something exciting, Harlan thought.

He did a little jig. He couldn't wait to run. He'd get to run real soon, right?

Of course, picking the exact route would have been easier if either of the individuals on their backs had actually had a goal in mind.

The wind out here had been picking up ever since they left the shelter of the trail running right next to the woodland that stretched from way above, covering the low mountains with a delicate veil of shimmering green, encroaching on the valley floor in sparse copses and the occasional lone pine.

There was space for it to pick up. Ever since they'd gone around the last turn, a bit of protruding forest of thick leaves and a mix of soft brown and black and white trunks, there was really nothing in the way between here and the desert gateway.

Well, aside from a lot of grass, lakes, rivers and such. Maybe it'd be better to say there was nothing too tall between here and there.

'It's the largest uninterrupted space in the Valley,' Erina informed him when Sam asked. 'Well, aside from the hills. If you're at the bottom of one all you can really see is grass, grass, and more grass.'

'How many do we have?' Sam asked.

'Hills?'

'Open spaces.

'Depends on your criteria,' Erina said. 'But if you go by things over a certain size, two.'

Not much competition there, Sam thought. Still, it was a respectable distance and not many places that looked like a picture postcard of summer in the alps could say that they sat right next door to a desert. An actual sandy desert, windswept dunes and all.

* No surprise there…

Sam didn't know how wide that was. He'd been explicitly told not to venture out into it. Passing through the gateway to the Sandsea was, he was informed, a one-way ticket to death.

Whether by dehydration or because you, eventually, fell over the edge, he wasn't sure. There was sweltering hot sand up here and there was equally roasting hot sand down there, all the way down on the planet's surface. How exactly the two were connected he wasn't sure. But it was a long way down and he had no interest in finding out the hard way.

It was peculiar, however, how the sand remained almost exclusively on the far end of the gateway, especially considering that the border between the two was more a break in the barren, rocky, mountains that surrounded them than anything else.

'I can hear you, you know,' Erina said. 'Stop grumbling. You said yourself we all needed to "get out" a bit after all the hard work this week. The stable is picturesque enough but the walls start growing on you after a while. This,' Erina spread her arms wide, 'this is about as "out there" as you can get — unless you want to start climbing Snowfell's little cousins or going to space. And I don't think the horses would be keen on *that*!'

Sam ignored the obvious sarcasm. It was practically how Erina communicated.

Either way, she wasn't wrong.

He let himself take in what lay before them. The grass covered hills seemed to stretch on forever, as long as he didn't turn around to look back towards where they'd come from. Bordering both were forests and mountains. Very thick forests, if his eyes were any judge. Old ones.

They could hide anything, they could.

They weren't very steep here; neither the hills nor the mountains. It didn't look unlike an ocean had been frozen in the middle of a storm. Ships would have had a … not very good time. The animals living here had no such problems. Their world remained safely solid and non-moving beneath their feet.

Still, plenty could hide in the dips between the hills. Whole marshes could have fit in between some of the larger ones.

Lots of things probably *were* hiding in the dips and troughs, Sam corrected himself. It wasn't as if they were looking out over giant herds of migrating quadrupeds.

It might be the first time he was out this far but he didn't need a lesson to know that. As large as the place was it wasn't *that* big. He couldn't imagine anything here having to migrate. Where would they migrate too? The other side of the mountain?

The saddle leather creaked as Erina leaned back, staring up at the clouds. White and fluffy they could have doubled as cotton candy had someone first dumped a bowl full of food colouring into the sky.

'Think we've gone as far as we can out here,' she said.

Sam raised an eyebrow at her. There wasn't anything here. They couldn't have come all the way out here for this, surely?

He didn't voice his question out loud, but he must have failed to concealed his confusion as well as he thought for Erina pointed towards the mountain that they'd skirted the outskirts of by travelling along the valley floor.

'We want to go up there,' she said. 'It'd have taken days to go through the forest from the other side, even if, on the map, it'd have been the shorter route.'

Sam's ears practically perked up. So there was a map? He'd have to remember that.

He shaded his eyes, looking up. It looked dense enough as it was. And this was the easy route? 'Was that the only reason?' he asked.

'That and the risk of getting lost.' Erina chuckled. 'You try to find where you are when in the middle of a forest and the only thing you see when you look up are leaves and branches.'

She made a face.

'Look on the bright side. It's an excellent thing to start out with for you. It's not tall or steep and we might even run into something interesting or two along the way.'

When Sam asked what she meant by "interesting" Erina didn't elaborate. Merely gave him one of those secretive, knowing, looks that he'd learnt meant he was likely to see something that defied explanation … again.

If he had to be completely honest, the view didn't look particularly mysterious. He'd seen similar ones elsewhere. The main difference he'd noticed so far was that here everything was sort of more … scrunched together. Not exactly a scientific term, but it felt appropriate.

While most of the mountains bordering the valley floor were covered with thick forests, especially at lower elevations, the ones behind those were more likely to be tall, barren, rocks. Even on those where you would assumed there should be vegetation there wasn't.

And if you kept going up, they'd be very cold rocks, very cold rocks indeed. Towards the north they were almost uniformly covered with ice or snow. Or ice *and* snow. They most certainly weren't blessed with an abundance of grass and trees — unless there was a species of ice-trees no one had told them about.

Sam wasn't the only one thinking along those lines. Erina was simply a whole lot more suspicious about it. Now that she thought about it, even in the lowest mountains, you'd find sparse patches, sometimes even large ones, where there should have been things growing, living, but there wasn't. Not even lichen.

The only time she'd caught sight of any animals there was when a lone stag had burst out of the thicket and raced across the empty, open space, trying to evade a predator. She'd heard chuffing, but never saw what had been chasing it.

She'd stumbled across a few of them by now. She didn't stay long, either. They felt … wrong. Like holes in … existence.

Which made no sense at all, but had all her actual senses screaming at her to leave and not come back.

She led Sam right to one of those now. Halfway up the side of the mountain and deep in a part of the forest so dense the horses could barely move at a walk.

They weren't keen on getting closer, either.

'My Lady?' Sam's eyes widened as, before them, the forest simply came to an end. A large, empty, circle the size of the landing pad for a medium spaceship, it smelled wrong. As if something was trying to creep up his nostrils, making them itch. The whole place felt wrong, for all that he couldn't explain what he was feeling. Something deep and large was burrowing into his inner self, yet everything around them looked perfectly normal*.

* Aside from, well, not being there…

Stomping his feet, Wave Rock snorted. Sam could feel the horse shiver. The dun really didn't want to be here.

'Figured showing you would be the only way,' Erina said. She tried to explain, lost herself halfway through and eventually just shrugged. 'Now you see why I keep telling you we always *go around*?'

'Indeed,' Seranthiem agreed. He felt the hairs on the back of his arms stand up.

'So that's what we do. You run into anything like this out there, big, small, doesn't matter. You back away and don't look back.'

'And mark them on the map, I presume?'

'No point,' Erina said. 'I call them Fairy Rings. Even the permanent ones only stay in the same general area not in one place. Most of them though, they disappear and reappear. Why? What do I know.'

Not the most scientific explanation in Sam's mind, but he wasn't about to argue. Whatever the reason behind it, neither of them wanted to find out the hard way what staying would do.

'So the forest grows back?' Sam asked.

'Once whatever this is, is gone? Yes. You'll find patches of relatively new trees all over the place. It doesn't seem to have any lasting effects, except, you know, slowly killing everything in it once it appears.'

'Charming.'

'Come on,' Erina said and nudged Harlan forwards, guiding him along the inner side of the ring. We get a bit higher and we might even get a bit of a view.'

'That would be … nice.'

Sam felt a bit of distraction would be welcome. Riding alongside the inner edge of the Fairy Ring made him feel uneasy. No wonder the animals avoided them.

'Let's pick up the pace a little,' Erina called over her shoulder. 'We don't want to stay here longer than we have to.'

Sam urged Wave Rock forward into a trot. The dun eagerly caught up to Harlan. There was safety in numbers.

What kind of lookout point had she been talking about, Sam wondered? It wasn't as if you could see the entire valley from *any* given point. No matter where you stood (except possibly on the very summit of Snowfell) could you make out *everything*[*]. The Valley and everything in it, valley floor, hills, mountains, marshes, even desert, twisted and turned like a very disorganized labyrinth with the hiccups.

Some stretches were hidden behind others. Some were concealed between lower mountains or taller hills. Some disappeared in the thick forests, dips in the ground that, from above, you didn't even notice were there. Others were simply lost behind taller peaks of some of the borderland mountains that had crept inwards just a little more than they should have.

Yet that wasn't anything compared to the rest of the world being, visually, locked behind that same border; the tall, inhospitable, peaks that surrounded the borders of the Valley itself. The outer rim. Outside of those there was nothing but a sheer drop for what must seem like an eternity should you be unfortunate enough to fall off the edge.

'Technically, you can see the sky,' Erina pointed out when Sam mentioned this, then frowned. 'Only it's not the same sky. Not exactly.'

'A mirror of a sky and the same sky at the same time?'

'Look, it's not like it can be scientifically measured. Trust me, they've tried. I'm doing the best I can with these explanations. I'm the only one who has been here. Well, and you, now.'

Sam learned that far, far to the east there were a small gap where barren ochre stone stacked and, creaking in the wind, gave way to the Sandsea. You could still see the mountains there. More so than you could here. At that point, it was about the only thing you could see. The forest and grasslands thinned out long before the rocks became dry and barren. In fact, the "mountains" were so close that they basically towered over you a few mere leagues, or less, away from what, elsewhere, would have been referred to as a mountain pass.

So far though Erina had been very mum about what lay beyond that … if anything. The border of mountains certainly stopped there and, supposedly, if you looked out all you could see in the distance were ripples in the air as the sky and ground came together in an ochre-blue hazy mist of heat.

[*] And even then things would have been hiding behind other things. That was geography for you.

‘Don’t go there,’ Erina said when he brought it up.

It certainly hadn’t sounded very inviting, so, so far, Sam hadn’t any intention of doing so. Now, he wanted to do so even less. The words had been spoken in the same tone, the same vein, that people used when they told you “don’t go swimming near the continental shelf. It’s a long way down and you have no idea what might be down there.[*]”

[*] Or, if you were a turtle person, “don’t go fall over the edge”.

DOWN DOWN DOWN*

Rivers sold separately. Terms and Conditions may apply.

Harlan stretched out beneath her. The trias stallion's stride lengthened, then lengthened again. Wind rushing past threatened to tear the breath from her mouth. Mane and tail whipped in it, black and white mixing together until the edge between them disappeared.

Even from a distance the bright red, white, and black horse stood out against the verdant green background.

It was too early in the summer for anything to have begun to dry. The grass beneath his hooves was soft and supple. Almost as fun to run on as to eat, Harlan thought.

Unlike in the fields, where everything sort of grew together, different grasses, flowers, herbs — up to his knees, sometimes — out here it was far more monotone. Not to mention short.

They were smooth, gentle, lapping hills that were barely more than a bump in the ground. The area around Fairy Lake wasn't flat, far from it, but this far out from the centre you'd be forgiven for asking why they were called "hills" at all. Here, where the forest thinned out and the plains began stretching out before you, it opened up the landscape and urged you to run, run, run.

Even the wind picked up out here. In the woods it had barely been a breeze rustling the top branches of the tallest ash and poplar trees. Now it was gathering strength, hitting you in the face with a fresh chill even in summer.

Though some of that might be due to the speed they were going at. Harlan was a lot of things but he wasn't slow. Not for a horse.

They came here enough that there actually was a proper trail through the forest. You could canter, but really letting loose? No. There were too many winding twists and turns for that.

Horse and rider alike enjoyed the speed. This close to the ground, moving with it, every step was another musical note in a symphony of freedom. On one side of them, the tree trunks were whizzing by.

'Faster. Faster,' Erina urged her mount on.

Not that Harlan needed it. The drumbeats of their hearts beat in tandem.

Loosening the reins even further, letting her horse run to his own desires, times like these reminded Erina of that Harlan "had" been a race horse. Or, more accurately, he'd been a horse she'd entered into the Phoenix Stakes. It hadn't been something like a proper profession.

She'd have a chance to compete there again, maybe — the invite only affair wasn't exactly going to throw their doors open to just anyone — but Harlan wouldn't. As a racer, rather than a rider, he'd had his chance. He'd lost. There would be no second chances.

If anything, out of all of them, Erina realized, the one most likely to enter that particular race again was Sam. He'd been the one riding in it the first time. She pushed the thought from her mind. There was plenty of other things she could do. Harlan could do.

She just needed to find them. Figure them out. What did you do with yourself when you had all the time in the world and no idea what to do with it? There was a reason why she kept herself so busy. The more practical things she had to deal with around the Valley the less time, and energy, she had to pursuing all those "what ifs".

She'd always been good at questioning herself above all others.

Harlan didn't care. While testing himself against other horses, not to mention the other creatures, the nightmares, that had been there, had been kind of fun, he much preferred this. No goal. No reason beyond running for the sheer joy of it.

The whole event, all the strange people, all the weird smells, all the *noise*. No, that wasn't for him. But this? This was something he would never tire of.

The stallion let out a loud whinny as Harlan sped up even more.

❋❋❋

Having spent the last couple of days living off rations — because camp cooking when you were alone was way too much effort — returning to High Fyelds came with several promises as far as Erina was concerned.

A proper bed was one. Proper food was another. Trotting into the yard, smelling mostly of horse, leather, and sweat, her nose didn't disappoint.

Erina sniffed the air expectantly, trying to catch the nuances of the scents that were drifting out from the kitchen. One thing was certain, the food at High Fyelds had improved dramatically since Seranthiem's arrival.

Not that she wasn't able to cook, when she remembered. Most of the time, when it was just her*, she just couldn't bother. Things like dinner took years to make, seconds to eat, and an eternity to clean up after. She'd rather spend the time doing something else. Anything else.

She did like eating, though…

Erina couldn't remember if "excellent chef" had been included on Sam's resume. Might not have been. A lot of things hadn't, now that she thought about it. Also, that kind of position hadn't been what he'd interviewed for.

So far there had proven to be several additional, but definitely not unwelcome, perks to his presence. If having to deal with another human being was simply the price she had to pay for delicious food, then so be it.

'Welcome back, My Lady,' Sam said over his shoulder, not taking his eyes off the skillet he was handling, as the main door creaked open. The door into the kitchen was open, allowing him to hear what happened in the rest of the house even if he couldn't see it.

'Thanks,' Erina replied. She dumped several saddlebags on the floor and shrugged off the satchel from her back, dumping it into a wooden chair sitting right on the inside of the front door.

'Smells wonderful,' she said.

'Thank you, My Lady.'

She knew better to interfere when Sam was cooking. It was the only time

* Which was, basically, all the time.

she'd ever heard him raise his voice. Erina grumbled, quietly, as to not let Sam hear her.

Apparently she "got underfoot". Which was a polite way of saying she was a damn nuisance in the kitchen.

'May I suggest you get cleaned up and an early dinner should be on the table when you're done,' Seranthiem said, his soft, clear, voice marred by the sizzling sounds coming from one of the pans on the range.

'Can't wait,' Erina said, retreating. 'My feet are killing me.'

'Right you are, My Lady.' Sam returned his concentration to the, right now, more important matter of not burning the food. He barely resisted a sigh when considering what he was having to cook *on*. But even with that he'd never live down the shame if he ruined the meal. Any meal.

The lack of electricity *was* a nuisance. There was no argument about it. There were all sorts of clever little ways of getting around that problem, true, but they required a different solution for everything. With electricity you just needed one, and a machine, and you could automate almost everything or, at least, make doing it a lot easier and less time-consuming.

Sam had a lot of time on his hands. That didn't mean he liked wasting it.

Erina had already spent a considerable amount of time researching the solution to lots of these little problems back before she couldn't even leave the Valley. Sam knew that.

He also knew that the Valley wasn't the only place in the Castician solar system where electricity didn't work. Or where it wasn't feasible to bring in permanent equipment. No matter how small battery pulls you had, they *always* ran out when you needed them most. It was one of the impermeable laws of the universe.

Still, the people visiting said places didn't want to do everything by hand. They needed their tools and things like shelters etc, to operate. In some cases because them not doing so was inconvenient. In some cases because them failing would mean the people would be dead.

Sam had already managed to acquire some devices along those lines and they were making his life a lot easier. High Fyelds already had a plethora of larger adaptions set up — there was no way Erina was going to do things by hand if she didn't have to — but Seranthiem felt most of those were for the stable and the house in general and very little in terms of working around the kitchen.

While the food made on the ancient iron range tasted absolutely delicious, it was a pain to use. Especially in terms of how long it took to set up and actually then use (not to mention clean), seeing how it required constant supervision. He had better things to do with his time than that.

It wasn't as if he could delegate the task to someone else. While he trusted his horse, Wave Rock suddenly turning into a top chef's assistant was one of the less likely things his imagination had ever surprised him with.

Sam wondered if he could convince his new employer to find them something more suitable. Or, at the very least, more flexible. Hiring more people was, probably, out of the question.

True, she didn't like to cook herself, but she did like to eat cooked meals. The more time he spent here, the less time he spent on other work around the stables, outside. Or with his books.

Yes, it would be a sensible idea. He would have to ask right away. Right away *after* dinner, that was. He'd heard the stomach growls when Erina had arrived. Negotiating on an empty stomach was a foolish choice at best.

As promised, dinner had been delicious. Afterwards they'd retreated to the living room. While cake had not been provided, there had been some excellent cookies.

Erina was happily munching on her third while listening to Sam's recommendations. She wasn't sure why he thought she'd argue with him. He knew more about the subject matter than she ever would.

True, it'd take a bit of effort. But it always did when she had to bring in things from outside the Valley.

'As long as you don't mind waiting until the next "supply run",' Erina said.

'Of course, My Lady,' Seranthiem made a small bow.

'Did you make a list? Why am I asking? Of course you made a list. Why don't you go write it in something other than short-hand and we can add them to the planner.'

'Right away.'

Sam hurried away, eager to see which things he'd be able to get once he'd shown it to her.

Erina glanced up to where, over the fireplace, hung the not-sword that she'd cobbled together all those years ago when she'd first crash-landed in the Valley. It was, in comparison to an *actual* sword*, clearly a vaguely sword shaped piece of durasteel. Her hands ached at the memory of having needed to sharpen it enough so that it could do its job.

Still, it had been all she'd had back then and it had gotten her out of more than one pickle. Also handy for cracking nuts with the hilt, which was more or less just a slightly thinner part of the same bit of metal wrapped in *a lot* of things to stop it from shearing your hand from your body when you picked it up.

As cumbersome as it had been, the sight made her smile. It was old and familiar and seeing it up there was, somehow, comforting. By now it was as much part of High Fyelds as any of the buildings or fields.

Since those days she'd not only invested in a proper sword, but actual lessons in using it. While there was nothing like necessity to make you learn fast on your own, there was something to be said for having someone teach you rather than by learning via impaling your own foot. It went faster for instance and was a whole lot less painful.

She'd needed to leave the Valley for all those things. A popular holo-instructor wasn't exactly something you could just throw up in a room here. What technology worked around these parts was always a matter up for debate. But it was usually safest to assume that anything with an electric current in it wouldn't.

And some things that did work didn't work all the time. That was the more infuriating part, in her mind. At least the other things you learnt not to rely on or even think about after a while. There was nothing like turning on the kettle with the promise of a nice cup of tea, only to find it stutter out a "nope, not today … sucker".

Whatever the rules here were, they were more than arbitrary, Erina had decided. It was more like being in a paddleboat lost in a rushing rapid and

* Made by someone who *actually* knew what they were doing.

steered by a very temperamental toddler who'd just thrown the last oar overboard.

Shaking her head at the folly of it all, including her choice of sticking around, Erina grabbed her favourite of the new blades and headed out. She might as well get some practice in while waiting.

Not all that much time later, wiping the sweat off her brow, Erina wondered if it was too late to talk Sam into participating. He should be showing up any minute now.

'How long does it take to make a list?' she asked the slender blade in her hand. 'He didn't decide to go around *the entire stable* and make notes, did he?'

Actually, the latter was definitely not impossible.

After several rounds with the very stationary make-shift training dummy, Erina took a break.

'This would be so much more fun with a sparring partner,' she wheezed as she tried to collect her breathing. Bending over she kicked up the sword where it had skidded off to.

'I always end up overdoing it, don't I? It's not like the air is going to try and strike me back, you know, dummy.'

As if realizing what she'd just said, her eyes turned to the innocent sky and frowned, just in case it *did* get any ideas. This *was* Darklight Valley after all. You never knew who was listening.

'Don't you dare,' she said wagging a finger in its general direction.

If the air did send any opponents her way they remained completely invisible and entirely non-combatant. Unless it was the sort of battle you didn't know you were having … until you lost.

'See? Utterly useless,' Erina muttered. 'Might as well get back inside.'

She'd barely made it into the living room before there was an almighty crack and rumble and the next thing she knew, the floor had disappeared.

Well, technically it didn't exactly *disappear*, it was still there. It was just no longer recognizable as a floor and had taken the express route down one story.

Despite a last minute dive towards the doorway, Erina went down with it.

In hindsight, maybe that dare from before hadn't been such a good idea after all? Erina would have to lodge a complaint, as soon as she figured out who, or what, to complain to. Also, it was hard to think straight when every bit that was you was complaining loudly at *you*. The word her entire body was looking for was "ouch!"

'What the rach did just happen?'

Erina blinked, trying to see through the grey dust that was, slowly, settling down to cover everything. Where was she?

Peering upwards, the particles in the air stung her eyes. She could just about make out it being lighter upwards then sideways.

'Where am I? Since when did we have a basement?'

Pushing off some of the debris that had, along with her, gotten lodged against a stone pillar, most of it seemed to be wood that hadn't disintegrated into dust. Guess she knew where all that came from then. And why it hadn't squashed her flat.

Getting to her feet unsteadily it seemed she was all there. Patting herself there were a few warm, wet, patches. 'That explains why my head is ringing,' she muttered, looking down at her hand, now smeared with red. 'No broken bones? Good. At least it wasn't the ceiling collapsing on me, I'd have been a gonner. Ow!

She yelped as, slipping and sliding on the unsteady piles of now rubbish, her foot set off a small landslide, sending a bunch of broken bits of building and furniture crashing down onto the floor.

'Where the blazers am I?'

Okay, technically she knew exactly where she was. She had, after all, moments before, been standing not but a few meters above where she was now. She could still make out the light from one of the lamps on the wall now that the air was beginning to clear up.

She coughed into the sleeve of her shirt, then kept holding it in front of her nose and mouth. Whatever was floating around in the air here, it was making her throat itch something terrible.

'Wasn't the whole building then? Suppose I should be grateful for small favours. One collapse at a time, please. Is that what you think I'd be saying?' Erina threw an angry glare into the shadowy twilight that surrounded her.

It had now gone from being almost pitch black with a sort of grey yellow tint, to having actual light shining down from above.

'Guess from down here the ceiling really did fall in,' she muttered. 'Fine. Fine. Sam? Anyone up there?'

Shouting didn't bring the rest of the house down, thankfully. Though, judging from the echo, there might be a lot more of said house than she'd previously realized.

It did bring a concerned looking Seranthiem leaning, carefully, over the edge. Though the sound of the entire floor caving in had probably done that already.

'Everything alright, My Lady?' Sam called down from above.

'Sam, is that you?'

It was a rather stupid question all things considered, but Erina couldn't stop herself. It escaped her mouth before she even knew what she was saying. The voice did sound more echo-y than usual. Guess the space down here was larger than the room above had been.

'Well, this was unexpected,' Sam said as he looked down at where, the last time he'd seen it, the living room floor had been.

Had been, was the operative word here. The wooden floorboards had been replaced by a, very dark, hole. It wasn't a hole in the floor. The floor was gone. Utterly. Completely. As was every piece of furniture. Except those on the walls. And the walls, obviously. And the ceiling.

His employer … not so much. The floor could be repaired with some time and attention. Squashed humans were rarely afforded the same privilege. Thankfully, the human version of an inkblot didn't usually call out to you. If they did, it wasn't for long and it certainly wasn't coherent. If they were, you should probably start running.

Erina sounded very much alive. It was kind of hard making out anything below, though.

The tall, silver-haired, man frowned as he kept trying to penetrate the void with equally grey, but very concerned, eyes. Teetering on the edge in the doorway was hardly proper behaviour in the circumstances. But he was not about to leap down into the nothing without at least knowing there was a way back.

'Your capacity for calmly stating the blatantly obvious never ceases to amaze me!' came from below.

While distorted by the stony echoes of whatever was down there it was also very much pissed off. A fact Sam attributed to it less because of the owner's ability to speak and more because every syllable was positively dripping with sarcasm.

Good. He hadn't looked forward to leaving this job so soon. He'd just started finding his feet here.

'Do you wish me to help you up, My Lady?' he asked, when, after a moment, there were no further acerbic comments from below.

'No. I'm having the time of my life here. Met some lovely chaps down here called Grout and Beam. Getting really well acquainted with broken bits of wood and stone was *so* on my list of things to do today!'

Sam bit back the chuckle threatening to rise in his throat at the response. Guess he didn't need to wonder if his employer were alright. She seemed to be in good spirits, all things considered.

He calmly started counting. He hadn't even gotten to four before a follow-up appeared from below.

'Of course I want you to bloody well help me up!' Erina shouted. 'I can't fly! This thing's a lot deeper than you'd think. Can you see anything? I think you're sort of a blurry shadow from where I stand.'

'Not much,' Sam admitted. 'The air should settle soon. Please wait while I retrieve some rope. I do believe I saw some longer rolls in storage.'

There was a vague echo-y, 'Oh, don't hurry on my account,' in response.

It wasn't long before a sturdy rope had been affixed to a heavy bedframe now pushed tight against one bedroom door. It would have happened sooner but Sam had needed to go back for a second rope after the first one had ended up being too short. He had accounted for the possible distance down, not having to thread the line of hemp through half the house to find something sturdy enough to tie it to.

'Stand by, rope away!' Sam shouted and flung the loose end over the side of the jagged edge.

Sam let a small flicker of displeasure swim across his delicate features. Up until today he'd considered the floor in the living room quite sturdy. While wood wasn't the hardest material around[*] this particular one was supposed to sit on top of bedrock.

Bedrock was known for not, generally, collapsing beneath your feet. That's why people liked building things on it.

Between a combination of climbing and pulling, Erina soon heaved herself over the edge. Sam backed up. There was only so much room in the doorway.

'Lovely. Just lovely,' Erina muttered as she dusted herself off, but there was no mistaking the almost manic grin where her face used to be.

'You're hurt,' Sam pointed out, indicating the injury that had coloured half her face red.

'What? Oh, yeah. That.'

'Would you like me to fetch the first aid kit?'

'It stopped bleeding. Don't think there's too much to worry about. I can get cleaned up later.'

There was something about the way she said that. Oh dear, Sam thought. What have I gotten myself into this time? Erina smiling usually meant someone was about to have a very bad time and it wasn't going to be her.

'You seem to be in good spirit, My Lady,' Sam said, casting an eye down to where she'd half climbed, half dragged herself up from. 'All things considered.'

'Grab some gear and some sort of torch, Sam,' the small blond said. 'I'm going back down there. And when I say "I", I mean "we". I suggest you change your clothes to something more suited for,' there was the briefest pause before Erina continued, 'spelunking about in mysterious caves?'

It had sounded like a question. It hadn't been one. Seranthiem's delicate nose twitched. There was no holding back the dismay this time. Sam shuddered at the thought — his expression almost perfectly mirroring that of a dog that had suddenly been told his favourite toy was going to go live with grandma now.

He coughed delicately. 'This isn't *quite* what I imagined when you said the High Fyelds needed remodelling,' Sam confessed. The briefest hint of disapproval flickered across his otherwise serene features.

[*] Though the people trying to build a spaceship out of semblance wood might have a thing or two to say about *that*.

‘A bit unexpected, true,’ Erina admitted. ‘But isn’t this exciting?’

No, not even a little, Sam wanted to say. He didn’t.

‘Shall we then, My Lady?’

Erina grinned. ‘Let’s go explore!’

They didn’t get far that first time. If nothing else, growling stomachs made them turn around. It was one thing to make camp when out adventuring but when there was a whole kitchen only a few minutes away — technically speaking — you were a lot less inclined to do so.

‘First thing in the morning,’ Erina said when Seranthiem asked if they were going back after having had a proper, if cold, dinner.

‘Really?’ Sam raised an eyebrow.

‘Not *that* early,’ Erina immediately clarified.

‘Best to put this away for now, then,’ Sam said, putting down the second set of clothes he’d picked up. He finished stashing a sparse selection of what Erina cheerfully referred to as “adventure awaits gear” into a worn, khaki coloured, satchel and slung it over his shoulder.

They might not need it right now, but he wasn’t going to leave it out here over night. He could hang it over one of the chairs in his bedroom.

‘Think someone’s going to steal it?’ Erina asked.

‘Here?’ Sam gave her an incredulous look. ‘I would not place a bet against that with those odds, My Lady. We might not have human thieves lurking in the night. That doesn’t mean things can’t go missing. There are a number of ordinary animals that will make off with your belongings if they think they’re interesting enough. Even hyraxes will get into your pack if you don’t secure it.’

And even if they didn’t steal anything, they’d always leave a mess. Seranthiem liked his things organized. It was comforting knowing where everything was at all time.

With that in mind, being here, at High Fyelds, he should have been tearing his hair out by now. Even on a typical, average, day, things rarely stayed in the place he expected them to.

Sam scoffed at himself internally. At this rate he was going to become as contradictory as Erina already was. Was that what you called a bad influence?

One thing he could always be sure of: life at the stables were rarely, if ever, boring. Not for him, at least. Erina seemed to be able to complain about boredom right in the middle of an adventure that she *enjoyed.*

A small smile tugged at the corners of his grey eyes as he glanced into what remained of the unprofessionally demolished living room as he walked past on his way to rest for the night.

❋❋❋

'Well, I'm no architect but I don't think this is a cave,' Erina said, her voice drifting up from below.

The next morning, after the chores had been done and the horses had been fed and cared for, the two of them had headed into what remained of the living room. Well, into the doorway of the living room. Mostly it had been Sam looking over Erina's head, which wasn't hard given that he was very tall and she was very short.

They'd coiled the rope she'd climbed up last night on the floor, well away from the edge. They'd exchanged a look as it was suggested they should leave it dangling, at which point they had both burst out laughing.

Yeah, that wasn't going to happen. There were no rubble walls to climb up from but, just in case some demon frog came crawling out of the darkness down there that thought ropes were overrated, they'd dragged a cupboard in front of the door.

At the moment, Sam was leaning over the edge staring into the uninspiring hole. There was plenty of edge. There was plenty of hole. There was very little floor.

'Everything alright down there, My Lady?' Sam called out.

It sounded like a surprisingly tight space now compared to when he'd stood on the edge last night but it still had that stony echo to it. As if the space was just a little bit bigger than it looked.

'Just peachy,' came from below. 'Looks safe enough. Can you get down here?'

'What a curious question, My Lady,' Sam said as, with catlike grace, he landed effortlessly on his feet. By the looks of it, climbing down the rope hadn't even been an effort.

The only thing ruffled on that man, even after everything, Erina decided, were the creases in his light blue checkered shirt. And even those were quickly smoothed beneath his hands as he turned and politely looked in the direction she was pointing.

I wonder if he even knows he's doing it? Erina found herself asking, silently. So far, if she was any judge, the answer to that was no.

'Colour me crazy,' she drawled, waving a hand over the general state of the rubble down here. Debris wasn't the only thing around. It was, if anything, merely taking up a bit of floor space in the grand scheme of things. 'Last time I checked caves weren't made of blocks of stone.'

She held up the green glass lamp Sam had lowered down earlier, trying to peer into the darkness around them to its warm flicker. They had glow sticks, but those were for emergencies. Which this wasn't.

'Times like these, I really do miss that good ole electricity,' Erina grumbled. 'Didn't someone invent bioluminescence lamps a few years back? We really should see about picking some up next supply run. Look.'

Taking in what the octagon lamp illuminated with its small candle, Seranthiem gently reached out and moved her much smaller hand up and down, watching the changing patterns on the walls.

Erina was right. This was no cave.

'If you want the lamp you can just ask you know,' Erina chided him gently.

'It's fine,' Sam replied, absentmindedly. He was already mulling over the possibilities of where they'd ended up. It definitely wasn't natural. But who could have built it? He'd never seen any ruins in the Valley, unless you counted the huge half-collapsed old megalithic "circle" out on the plains.

'This is quite unexpected,' he said, after nearly a minute's silence between them which Erina hadn't been inclined to fill. 'I gather you did not know it was here?'

Erina snorted. Of course he'd ask the obvious question, wouldn't he? Covering all the bases. Reliable. That made her more at ease.

'Sure I did,' she said. 'Didn't you see the huge warning sign at the gate? "Welcome to High Fyelds. Watch out for the dropping floors!"

'Hmm…'

'Hmm at you too.' Erina shook her head. She should have known better than to think something that simple would faze him. 'I checked it out earlier. This goes further in. Come on, let's see what's down there.'

At least it was easy to see what was around them. It wasn't like they'd be exploring the place for hours and hours and getting lost in the process. That was if they stuck to the main opening beneath the now demolished living room.

They didn't.

'There seem to be several, dare I say doorways, leading out of this chamber,' Sam said.

'Even more if we tried digging through that,' Erina said, poking at where one of the doors in one of the chambers down here was completely blocked by rock and soil packed so tight that if you'd been upstairs it would have made a decent field to plough and plant corn in.

'I think not,' Sam said.

'Let's try, hmm, that one?' Erina pointed into a random rectangle of darkness. What little light they had reflected of what must be another, smaller, room just beyond.

'After you.'

As they traversed the, seemingly, abandoned space down here, there were no sounds other than what they brought with them. No light other than their lamp.

There were, however, smells. Mostly it smelled like a closet that had been locked up for years and years. Dry. Dusty. Old. Very old.

'I wonder how long this have been down here?' Sam mused. He ran a gloved finger over the carved stone. He was whispering. Any time either of them raised their voices they had to wait for the cold echoes to stop before the other could reply.

Spooky *and* inconvenient, as Erina put it.

'Since it was build, I'd guess.'

'You *know* what I mean, My Lady!' Sam said reproachfully.

'You know, it's strange,' Erina said. 'It sounds a bit like we're under water, except we're not.' Lifting the lamp a little higher, towards the ceiling, she looked up. 'See that. How thick do you think that is? Why didn't we ever catch any echoes from down here through the floor if it *was* hollow?'

'I honestly don't know,' Sam replied.

In hindsight, Erina thought that them *not* having heard any weird sounds while walking around down here was what should have made them suspicious. The Valley was *the* place where things were never what they seemed*. It definitely didn't follow the rules, especially not those pesky natural laws.

'I remember you telling me that the stables were built on an old ruin,' Sam mused, in wonder. 'I didn't realize they were going this far down.'

'Me neither, Sam.'

That was the thing. At first they'd assumed what they'd landed in had once been some sort of basement. That suggested the floor was flat. It wasn't.

Not that the incline was steep. If anything it was barely noticeable, but as they kept edging forward through the various rooms — most of the doors having been lost to age, if they'd ever been there to begin with — the feeling that something was off was beginning to creep in. In some of the rooms, one side of the walls became a constant, actual, wall of stone. As if they'd stepped into a giant cave sealed off by level after level being built around it.

There were remnants that suggested that this space had once been far more extensive than the small bit they were exploring. Most of the doorways were blocked, either by rocky debris or by earth packed so solid it was halfway on the road to becoming stone.

'We appear to be going "around" something,' Sam pointed out. 'Something very large, given how little the wall curves.'

'I suppose there goes the "earthen cellar" theory,' Erina said. 'No sign of anything having been stored down here so far. No sign of anything, really. Whoever lived here must have really cleared house when they moved out or they were big into the minimal aesthetic.'

That was as good an explanation as any, Sam supposed. Even at a cursory glance there was nothing on the floor but stone dust and nothing on the walls other than the odd stains. Didn't places like this at least have a broken pot in the corner or something?

'Some red marks on the stone could be remnants of iron torch-holders,' Sam said. 'But other than that I think you're right. Nothing. Even ancient civilizations usually leave something behind.'

* Maybe one of the reason why she felt so at home here?

'Only in the history books, Sam,' Erina chortled. 'On Casticia we don't really do history. Not of the planet, anyway. We haven't exactly been here long,' she added, dodging out of the way of a scandalized not-quite glare.

'The Cataclysm didn't leave much behind, that much is true,' Sam agreed.

'We don't even know what that means. It's just a fancy name they came up with because they can't imagine there wasn't anything here before.'

'Which means this could be the oldest known structure on the planet. The only one. Certainly the only one still standing.'

'It's not standing,' Erina shot back. 'It collapsed. *My* living room at that!'

'I believe we've reached some form of antechamber,' Sam said, smoothly changing the subject.

'In the *basement*?' Erina quirked an incredulous eyebrow in her companion's direction.

But why not? It wasn't as if either of them knew what this place had *really* been.

'Other suggestions are most welcome, My Lady. Indeed, I'm all ears.'

Erina huffed. She'd have to pay him back for that one later. Much later. When he definitely wouldn't expect it. Right now she was getting hungry. They'd been walking around down here for hours. Good thing they'd made sure to mark their way. It might not have been meant to be a maze when it was built, but that's certainly what it felt like in the dark.

And cold. All this stone and underground, she wished she'd brought an actual jacket. Brrr.

'Antechamber to what exactly, Sam? There's nothing here. Might as well go back and try one of the other paths.'

'It bears all the hallmarks of one,' Sam insisted. 'I don't believe this is a dead end.'

'You're the history-buff,' Erina said. 'But unless there's a secret door somewhere, it seems very end-y to me.'

'It can't be.' Walking over, Sam, who'd borrowed the lamp, while keeping himself on the outside of the last doorway they'd found, put the hand with the light in it through said door.

Erina was right. It seemed empty. There was also something … different about it. He couldn't quite tell why he was so certain it was important. Maybe because someone had, it seemed, gone through a great deal of trouble making it look so ordinary, so dull, that you passed it by without even thinking.

People rarely did that without reason. Good reasons. It *had* to be hiding something.

This chamber was old even when compared to the structure they were already standing in. That was the feeling that was radiating from it. Age. Not the age that came with crumbling, slowly dying. No, this was something else.

There wasn't really anything physically there to support the idea, but he could feel it. Glancing over at his companion, though she clearly tried to pretend otherwise, it was clear she, too, was feeling it — whatever *it* was.

A breath held. Whispers of ancient times long since passed. A memory returned. The hint of a promise.

Whatever the conditions down here had been over the, quite frankly, incomprehensible, amount of time that must have passed since last a living soul set foot in this chamber, they were clearly not the same as the ones that had allowed Father Chronos to reign supreme through the rooms and passages they'd walked through to get here.

Logically and scientifically nothing here should still have been standing, knowing what the Cataclysm had done to the planet itself. Even without that, the eons that had passed since then would have been enough to wipe any trace off the surface.

Judging by the testimony of their eyes as the flickering light lit up the room beyond, logic and science had evidently been given a red card and been made to go sit in a corner.

Though calling it a "room" might be a bit overly generous.

'It's more of a cell, really,' Erina commented. She pushed past Sam and walked into the room.

There was a sort of a tingle as she stepped over the threshold. As if, for the briefest moment, she was pushing against something that didn't want them to enter.

'This is … different,' Sam admitted, as he followed. He held the lamp up high. The cell was so small that it lit up all walls equally, leaving shadows dancing only in the corners of the ceiling.

'You don't say,' Erina nodded. She narrowly avoided stepping on Sam's foot as she turned around. 'Sorry, not much space.'

Well, she wasn't wrong about that, Sam thought. The room that was more of a cell was barely enough for a large bed, if anyone had wanted to put one in here — meaning neither of them had any trouble seeing what it contained. They were just having a hard time adjusting to the idea.

Unlike when they'd looked in from the outside, the small stone room was no longer empty. Not … entirely.

Erina caught her companion's eyes. 'Well, they do say seeing is believing,' she said and shrugged. 'Weird place to put an altar, if you ask me.'

'In addition I *believe* there is no dust,' Sam said.'

'Some sort of stasis field, maybe?'

'Lasting this long?'

'Maybe not.'

They took a moment looking around but, no, other than the raised platform — which was looking suspiciously like an altar chopped in half and shoved into the far wall* — there was no other structures in here.

There were what looked like two columns, but they were carved into, or out of, the altar itself. Seeing how they barely reached above Erina's waist, they were the very opposite of big.

'Good thing they don't have to hold up the ceiling,' Erina quipped.

Sam tilted his head slightly to the right, examining what was in front of them. He tried comparing it to pictures he'd seen of old ones from Earth. It was a little … unimpressive.

'Is it an altar or merely a dais of some sort?' he asked.

'Your guess is as good as mind,' Erina replied. 'A bit bland for an altar if you ask me. Aren't they usually more ornate?'

'If it is, it's too clean to have been of the sacrificial type … most likely. Too small.'

'Could have been very small sacrifices,' Erina, who had a far darker imagination than Seranthiem, suggested. 'Like mice. Bit hard to tell with all that scrunched up cloth on top, to say nothing about the huge book.'

Sam's voice took on an affronted edge. 'Sacrificing books *would* be a sacrilege. But I don't think that's what's happening here.'

* The definition of "far" being a matter up for debate.

If it was dedicated to something, there was no evidence of it. No carvings of any kind. It would have looked good with two large candelabra on either side, Erina thought. As it was, it seemed as if the large — very large — thick tome was bound in some sort of unrecognizable dark brown leather with even darker speckles. Whatever hide this had been made from, it was no animal Erina knew of.

The one other thing to note, aside from its sheer size, was how it was held shut by two, thick, leather straps threaded into ornate, metal, buckles.

'What do they think the pages are gonna do?' Erina asked. 'Escape?'

As entertaining as books could be, they weren't alive. Not outside fiction, at least.

Ignoring the background noise of Erina's musings, Sam reached out and touched the book. First with a writing stylus he pulled from one of his pockets (you could never be too careful and the whole set up practically screamed "trap"). Giving it a gentle poke, it didn't as much as wobble.

His investigation came up short despite the suspiciously placed curio. His face got closer and closer as he tried to catch every detail. It did mean he got good look at the faint, but highly intricate, designs etched into the leather.

Neither of them had seen them from a distance. As Sam pointed them out, what they'd both first taken to be shadows revealed the images behind. Mere lines, yet appearing so, so alive.

'It would have taken someone considerate time and skill to bind and decorate this,' Sam said.

He explained that books, tomes, really, of this type were rarely seen outside of museums if they were pre-arrival. It certainly was a long time since he'd handled one and none of those came even close to the age of this thing, for all it didn't look a day over a hundred.

As such, he handled it almost reverentially. Picking it up with delicate, pale, fingers, he studied the pattern, hoping to discern some clue of its origin without first having to open it.

Unless someone very dedicated had hidden away a Big Book of Botany (for the flowing lines formed shapes that were, in his mind, supposed to evoke the impression of climbing vines and leaves and animals leaping through them) the cover didn't betray the book's content at all.

Turning it over, the design was mirrored on the back, with the exception for that there weren't any buckles.

How old was it? It had to be ancient. Beyond ancient. From before the Cataclysm. That was years counted in numbers that were, quite honestly, beyond comprehension. A thousand years, there you had something to compare. Built structures could last that long. But when time started to become measured in megaannums… It was the timescape of planets. Not books.

It didn't look that old. It didn't feel it, either, if his fingers were any judge. The leather was a little dry but no more than he'd have expected from something left in the open like this.

Holding up the tome, he took a couple of careful sniffs.

It didn't smell wrong. There wasn't any of that, almost stale, musty, dry scent that any well cared for old books always carried with them. And there wasn't even a hint of the "damp, been around the block" smell.

If anything, handing over the lamp to Erina, he was now almost completely absorbed. With a delicate touch he managed to unbuckle the tome and open it. The paper, parchment really, didn't crinkle anything like what he'd have expected.

'Should I leave the two of you alone?' Erina asked, one eyebrow raised.

She didn't get a reply … or even acknowledgement that he'd heard her. He probably hadn't, she realized. He seemed utterly enthralled.

The pages turned easily as Seranthiem began flipping through them. They moved almost enthusiastically. Each page felt thick, the ink barely bleeding through even when he held it up to the light. This wasn't a book of secrets. It *wanted* to be read.

Intrigued, momentarily even forgetting to wonder why the strange script that flowed over the pages — with the occasional stain, inkblot and some smudges here and there it clearly hadn't been penned by a scribe — was something he could even read, never mind understand.

Sam was soon lost in the tale the book told. Even from the very beginning he gathered it was some sort of chronicle. But of what? The story drew him in, making him a part of it.

'Sam? Hello?'

Erina waved her hand up and down — the one not holding the lamp — but there was no response from her companion other than a sort of vague, 'Hmm,' which she couldn't tell if it was meant for her or the book.

She'd heard of getting absorbed in stories, but this was a bit much. Oh well, at least the thing wasn't literally absorbing him. If it suddenly grew teeth and tried to eat his face she was more than ready to smack it into a wall. When such shenanigans failed to materialize, she lost interest.

Erina shrugged. 'Fine. You do that,' she muttered. 'I'll go look for stuff.'

Not that there was anywhere to go. She could survey the entirety of the small chamber without barely having to turn her head.

At first glance, the stone dais didn't contain anything else exciting. Only after a while did Erina see what she'd been looking at the whole time. The cloth the tome had been resting on. It had appeared a bit ruffled before, but now it was just one smooth piece draped over the top of the dais, turning that grey stone into a deep, void-eating, black.

'Well, well, what do we have here?' she mumbled, rubbing her hands together. 'This is more like it.'

While the book might have stolen all of Sam's attention, to Erina this looked much more interesting. Not that she'd been surprised. Not really. Even with as little time as they'd spent together she'd already learnt that Sam and books was a lost cause. To the serene, silver haired, man they might as well have their own gravitational pull. If there was something readable anywhere, you could be sure you would find, eventually, Seranthiem there.

But this? Unlike the dry pages of any book, this rustled beneath her fingers even as she ran them across the surface while it still sat, snug and on display, on the top of the stone.

It felt as if handling something very old back when it had first been made. Your mind told you it was one age, but all your senses told you something else entirely.

Picking it up, it unfolded, unfurled, like a river cascading over her hands, through her fingers. What had looked like a single layer revealed more and more fabric as she held it up higher and higher. Giving it a good shake out, it wasn't unlike staring into nothing (which might explain why she'd seen it but hadn't really registered that it had been there).

There was pitch black. There was vanta black. And there was this. It was black in the way that it didn't only seem to drink in the shadows around them but, somehow, reflect them back, pulling even your senses into itself.

'Hey, check this out!' Erina called out.

'Hmm? What? Oh, yes, certainly.'

It took a moment, several even, for Sam to register he'd been asked a question. No, been given a request.

'I don't think you should be touching that, My Lady,' he said without even looking up from the story he was, by now, oh so engrossed in. It was just getting interesting.

Erina made a displeased sound at the back of her throat. 'You're one to talk,' she said.

Sam gingerly turned another page.

'Seems to be some sort of clothing,' Erina said. At first she'd presumed it was a blanket, there was just so much material. 'Might be a coat or robe maybe?'

She kept muttering to herself as she turned the constantly escaping piece of cloth over, trying to find where it started.

'It's too big for you,' Sam pointed out, finally glancing up, as if he just knew what she was thinking.

He wasn't wrong, though, Erina had to admit. She grimaced. Even holding it up as far as she could, stretching her arms way over her head, the bottom still dragged on the floor. A lot.

Whomever had worn this had been tall. Really tall.

Or, alternatively — and a far less enjoyable thought — she really was that short.

'It'd probably fit you,' Erina said. 'I think. Want to try?'

'Thank you, My Lady, but no,' Sam replied, his head already lost behind the covers once more.

Realizing that his attention was elsewhere, Erina shrugged. 'Oh well, no harm in trying.'

After fiddling around with the smooth material, eventually finding a sleeve, she stuck one arm in, then, with a bit more struggle, the other.

The black cloth draped around her like an oversized python around a squealing hyrax. A ridiculous amount was now gathered around her feet. An excellent tripping hazard. Not that she had any plans to move.

'This must be what it feels like trying on your parent's clothing as a small child,' Erina mumbled to herself.

'Hmm?'

'I think you might be right,' Erina said, looking over her shoulder at Sam. 'It really is too big. Maybe we can hem it or something. Your find any more interesting? Has to be, right?'

'Quite fascinating, My Lady,' Seranthiem agreed, only paying partial attention. He nodded sagely, licked the tip of a finger, and turned another page.

'Sam?'

'Yes, My Lady?'

The words were clear, not mumbled, but even Erina picked up on how distant they felt. He seemed to be answering on automatic rather than by actually hearing what she'd said.

She gathered her voice, calling forth the same tone that made the animals around the Valley pay attention even when they didn't know her. You didn't need to understand the words. The intention was enough.

'Seranthiem?'

'Hmm?'

'*How are you reading that*?'

Sam's attention shifted slightly in favour of his companion, caught out more by the tone of her voice than the use of his full name.

'The same way you read all old books, My Lady. By .... Oh.... Oh, my...'

His voice dropped to the bottom of the floor along with his face as the realization finally caught up with him. *How* was he reading this? He stared down at the text in his hands.

'I should not be able to read this, should I?'

'A goodness knows how old book sealed away in a secret chamber in a ruin in the middle of nowhere sitting on top of an elevated column of rock that most people haven't even been able to see until recently?' Erina quirked an eyebrow at him. 'No. No you bloody well shouldn't.'

'My Lady!'

Erina had expected incredulousness, but while that was certainly where it had started, even between those short few letters it had already shifted to something else. Concern.

Sam nodded towards her, as if trying to gather her attention to something without actually saying anything. Without moving.

'Look down,' he said, giving up the attempt at silent communication.

Erina did so.

There was another soft, 'Oh.'

The robe fit her perfectly, ending just around her ankles. Now that wasn't disconcerting at all.

For the briefest moment worry gnawed at her, causing her blood to race. Then she shrugged. It didn't feel wrong.

'Oh well,' Erina said. 'Hardly the strangest thing that's happened in this place. Let's head on back, shall we?'

'Of course.' Sam quickly scanned the place, but there didn't seem to be anything else hidden in a dark corner somewhere.

MYSTERY

Exploring strange new places was pretty standard as far as Erina was concerned. Interesting, but nothing to get worked up about. Of course, she'd never counted on one opening up right under her own home.

Deep space or bedrock beneath her feet, that's what she preferred. Even so, once they'd determined that nothing else seemed to be in danger of collapsing, the only further interest she had in it was getting the floor fixed.

That was going to … be a while. In the meantime, they cleared out what little remained in the room itself. Sadly, a lot of important items and paperwork had been eternally lost to the big rubble pile in the sky.

Meanwhile, there were plenty of things to do around the stable itself. The most joy either of them got was when they got to leave. Both Harland and Rocky agreed, though not for the same reason.

Taking leisurely trips, there was a lot nearby that made for excellent nap spots. Extra tasty bushes and clumps of grass … for the horses, Erina wasn't about to volunteer to start eating grass. Relaxing walks through the leafy, inviting, forest that lay on the border of the stable.

More often than not, when going long distances, it was work related. That didn't mean you couldn't find things to enjoy along the way, just that there was a goal. Get there, do what you needed to, and get back again.

This time was no different.

As usual they had stopped before it got dark. While it was possible to set up camp (what little they bothered with) after dark, especially with the moons out, it wasn't ideal and it wasn't like they were pressed for time. If anything, time was the one thing they had in abundance.

Erina didn't care for it. The camping, that was. Neither did Sam, for all that he'd never complain about it out loud. If his employer insisted on something and it wasn't detrimental to either himself, his conscience, or the surroundings, he didn't argue.

Thankfully, in terms of flailing around in semi-darkness trying to find things, care for the horses, themselves, and not miss camping right next to a giant anthill — an unpleasant experience in the morning if anything — the two of them were in perfect agreement.

It would have been easier if they'd been able to use their dioms. But no. Sam had shoved his in a drawer after first arriving and hadn't bothered with it since. Now that he thought about it, he didn't think he'd gone so long without access to it in his life. Good thing he had an excellent memory. It'd be a pain if he'd needed to look everything up every time he had to do something, no matter how simple.

Why some tech worked here and some didn't (not to mention why some only worked *sometimes*) was anyone's guess. Sam had been trying to test it, but so far he hadn't been able to find a pattern.

'Temperamental,' that's what Erina called it. Usually she didn't even bother to try these days and simply assumed it wasn't going to work. It saved a lot of time and frustration.

Of course, when you discovered that something did work regardless, that made for twice the amount of frustration and annoyance. Both at the current time and thinking back at all the other ones when you could have used it.

Once you'd gotten into the habit of not thinking about it, though, it became more of an afterthought.

It made you extra grateful for the horses. Their presence and willingness to share their strength saved them having to do a lot of things solely by hand-power alone. Saved them having to walk everywhere, too.

There was no way Erina would have been traipsing around the Valley like she did if she'd had had to use her feet to do it, Sam thought.

Not that Sam minded walking. In fact, he rather enjoyed it. It was, however, a bit time-consuming when you had somewhere to be and not a long time to get there.

'Don't go wander off too far now,' Erina told Harlan as she removed the last of the tack by pulling the bridle over his ears.

The horse nickered. It was getting dark, what was he going to do? Wander off and break a leg in a hyrax hole or something?

Harlan tried to investigate his person's pockets for treats and, after getting shooed off with some chuckles, when none materialized, he walked over to where Wave Rock was grazing at what looked like a particularly delicious clump of field grasses.

Soon both horses were enjoying a pleasant evening meal, occasionally nibbling friendlily at each other's necks.

Some people suggested you didn't, if out and about, let your mount roam about on their own unless they were wearing some sort of halter or geotag. But "they" said a lot, Erina thought. It wasn't as if she'd ever figured out who this mysterious "they" were, anyway. Ineffable, that's what they were.

She hadn't gotten to where she'd been as a Cognitor by listening to what "they" said. Besides, this mythical "they" seemed to be about as useful as a towel in a power outage most of the time. Never mind when it came to this new life. Besides, she'd always figured you learnt a lot more by listening to what people *didn't* say.

Or said when they didn't think you could hear them. Or understand them. That one never got old.

Knowing their ways, their secrets, made it far easier to turn their own words against them. They didn't like that*.

Setting your horse lose and letting them roam free while camping was, probably, sound advice for most people. Erina had no problem admitting that much.

So far she hadn't encountered a single resident of Darklight Valley that could be labelled "most" of anything, people or otherwise. And that included herself.

* These weren't the same "they" as the previous ones. Probably.

If anything, Seranthiem was the most *normal* inhabitant around. And, personally, Erina doubted that anyone so put together was so through and through. That sort of presentation took effort. A lot of effort.

Not to mention self-control. Now there was something she had a lot of experience with. If she hadn't, life would have been a lot messier than it had been … and there had been plenty of messes through the years.

She wondered what Sam's story was.

One thing she *did* know already. When left to his own devices, Seranthiem was almost as much of a recluse as she was. He was just a lot more polite when getting his private space and time invaded.

That might not mean anything. Some people could smile sweetly while running a plasma-cutter through your spine*. She might wonder and speculate, but she wasn't about to go around asking. She wouldn't appreciate someone poking into her past, Erina certainly wasn't about to go do it to someone else … without good reason. And "I'm curious" was not a good reason.

'Come on, let's get everything set up,' Erina said. 'Not much time until it starts getting dark.'

There was plenty of time, Sam thought, carefully pulling things from the packs and setting them aside by the stones he'd collected to build the small fire inside.

There was no shortage of stones out here but being out of the forest meant there was less to fuel the fire. He'd taken one look where they were going and tied a small bundle of stripped branches to the saddlebags.

There were other things out here you could burn. He did not like them.

Soon enough the campfire was lit. Eating the evening's meal took almost no time at all. The dishes took even less, on account of there not being any — unless you counted the scrunched up foil that had been used to bake the piping hot potatoes in the red glowing coal.

Erina could still taste the slight hint of smoked charcoal from where hers had rolled away and into said fire while she'd been in the process of eating it. It had, true to form, singed her fingertips.

Leaning back against Harlan's saddle, it creaked a bit as cloth and leather

* Don't ask … just … don't.

rubbed against each other as she tried to get comfortable. Breaking open a sealed packet of dried puffmellows, she took a couple then offered the packet to Sam.

'Better eat some quick and hope Harlan doesn't wake up or he'll mob you for them,' Erina said.

'Puffmellows are hardly good for horses, My Lady,' Sam admonished her.

Erina chortled. 'Tell me something I don't know.'

'Hmm…' Sam threw a glance in the direction of where both their mounts were fast asleep. 'A fair point,' he said, softly.

'Sam?'

'Yes?'

'Did I ever ask if you could use a sword? I don't remember.'

Sam straightened up, refocusing on the task at hand; the question. That had been quite the change of topic. If she didn't remember asking, she definitely didn't remember what he'd replied.

Or it was a trick question. That wasn't entirely out of character. Over the course of his time here he'd learn that there was a great deal that his enigmatic employer didn't remember: like where she put the screwdriver two seconds ago or that time he'd found one of the loose snaffles in the cold storage despite her swearing up and down she hadn't been near that when she'd last used it.

For someone so clever Erina could be very not-quite-there at times.

'I do believe you did ask that, My Lady,' he replied calmly.

It was hard to tell if she was looking thoughtful or if she'd already drifted off somewhere else entirely.

The night had descended while they'd eaten. The sky, so limited in its palette during the day, had come alive with colour, light, and a depth that seemed to stretch into eternity. A clear night, the Ryumoto Nebula alternated between leaving parts of the sky in complete blackness, as if all stars had gone out, and bright, colourful, clouds that could turn into anything your imagination desired.

The night sky, depending on the hour, was anything but black dotted with pinpricks of light. At the moment, the turning of the planet meant the outer tendrils of the nebula had crept over almost half of the heavens, rendering a stark contrast between the two.

‘So?’

‘So, what, My Lady?’ Sam asked in return.

‘You answer?’

‘I said already, did I not?’

‘No, I don’t think you did.’

Ah, so she *definitely* didn’t remember, then, Sam thought. ‘Same as I will do this time, I believe,’ he said. ‘Yes, I do know how to avail myself of one. Would I be of any use in actual battle? Perhaps not. I imagine that would depend on what I’m be fighting.’

He’d long since gotten used to the convoluted ways of these discussions. Erina was an excellent example of a walking, talking*, contradiction.

On one hand she was quite capable of bluntly stating something and on the other equally likely taking ages to work around to what the actual topic of the discussion was — or what she was asking for — and that was if she didn’t get side-tracked along the way.

Interrupting her was a good way of doing just that. Sam had learnt to wait for long pauses to determine if she’d actually finished talking and was waiting for him to answer, for the next words to form, or had wandered off and started doing something else.

Waiting for the trains of thought to have all aligned on the tracks and been assigned a locomotive was the only way to make any conversation make sense. Derailing them merely meant everything took ten times as long and would, almost certainly, lead to Erina getting annoyed and frustrated.

Waiting didn’t require much effort. He was happy to.

‘Did I say something about needing to see that for myself?’ Erina asked, as she racked her brains for memories of the past conversation.

‘Not quite in those words, My Lady. But I gather that is what you meant.’

‘Well, no time like the present, don’t you think? I’ve got some trainers lying about…’

When Sam didn’t reply, it slowly dawned on Erina what she’d said. She coughed uncomfortably. ‘I mean, when we get back.’

‘Of course.’

‘I *do* remember telling you that blasters and their ilk don’t work here,’ she

* Maybe not so much talking … unless she had to. Not to other people.

said. 'I'm also pretty sure that I've never seen you fight. I just need to know you can defend yourself out there.'

'My Lady, I assure you … should the need arise…'

'Seranthiem!'

'Yes?'

'I told you, this place can be dangerous. And if something *did* happen, do you see a field hospital anywhere? No. If anyone of us get injured, all we've got at hand is what we've got at hand, are you following me?'

'Not … exactly,' Sam admitted.

'It means, if something happens, no one's going to come and save you … except me,' she added. 'If I know something happened and can get there fast enough that is. Trust me, I make a pretty terrible substitute for a doctor.'

Seranthiem hung his head. It looked like he wasn't going to get out of this one. He opted for the second best way out of the current dilemma. He changed the subject.

'It's truly spectacular,' Sam said, turning his eyes to the heavens.

This earned a scoff from his increasingly sleepy-looking companion. 'Pretty, sure,' she said. 'Far away from everything, yeah. Usually that's a good thing. When you want to go somewhere though it's a pain in the ass. And there's bugger all for entertainment.' Erina's grousing sounded unusually peeved.

'You could try singing, My Lady, Sam suggested. 'If you're that desperate.'

Erina huffed. 'Trust me, you *don't* want me to do that!'

'Believing in yourself is important.'

'True,' Erina agreed. 'And *I believe* I know that unless you want your ears to bleed, don't ask me to do any singing.'

Sam coughed, delicately. 'Perhaps not then.'

Whatever else his companion was, musically inclined was apparently not it. Eventually he'd find that out in person, and then seriously wish he hadn't.

Even Harlan, who would have curled up at her feet in front of the fireplace if he'd been able to, raced away should Erina be in a singing mood. This, praise be, was not to happen very often — and certainly not when she thought anyone could hear her.

Hence why Sam had never been subjected to that particular agonizing torment.

Thankfully, not even Erina could butcher humming … provided you weren't actually familiar with the tune.

❊❊❊

Their "trip" around this end of the Valley was into its fourth day when it happened. The noise.

Not the usual sort that you got out here in the wild. A weird sort of thumping clop sound.

Erina jerked her head up, like prey caught by an impetuous lion. Listening intently for anything suspicious, she remained almost entirely still, pulling Harlan to a halt, as if moving would cancel the sound out.

Not that the Valley was short on suspicious sounds in general. You got used to ignoring some pretty wild things that would have sent the alarms tripping in other places.

Oh, there's a giant cryptid that's attacking the cattle on the other side of the field you're standing in? Meh. Bullcow's got your leg? Just shake it off. A two-storey icicle shattered and now your back's full off melting shrapnel? Just another Tuesday.

Not that they had cows … of any sort. There were creatures that were sort of vaguely cow-related, if you squinted and stood a long way away. She *had* caught a glimpse of something that "could" have been a giant sea monster in one of the deeper lakes.

No fun it one of *those* started chomping on you, either. Or did those things have suckers? Maybe she was thinking of giant squid? Not like she'd seen enough of the thing to tell.

Mind you, it could just have been a log. A very wet, soggy, log that wasn't there the next time she blinked.

This sound, it was like that. Enigmatic.

'What was that?' Erina shot at Sam, turning around in the saddle, trying to get his attention.

'What was what, My Lady?' Seranthiem asked. Wave Rock had to walk backwards to "catch-up" with the other pair.

'That. Can't you hear it?'

At first he had no idea what she was talking about. He didn't hear anything other than the regular summer sounds. The buzzing of insects. The birdsong. The whinny from up ahead where one of the wild herds was having a staring contest with the big eagle that had followed them for the past two hours.

The trias reared, mane blowing in the wind.

'Easy there. Down boy,' Erina encouraged him. 'There's nothing scary out here … I think.'

Sam scanned their surroundings. His eyes didn't pick up anything out of the ordinary. Neither did Wave Rock's apprehension. The dun stallion flicked an ear, which was about as high of an opinion he had of Harlan's antics. Whatever it was, it clearly didn't bother him.

Then the sound came again. Or, at least, Sam presumed it was the same sound. Not having heard it the first time it wasn't like he had anything to compare it with.

It was … odd. A sort of dull thud. Repeated dull thuds coming from … somewhere.

It couldn't be far because it was barely audible. If he and Erina had been talking, between that and the horses walking there was no chance they'd have heard it.

But where was it coming from?

Turning his head this way then that, Sam again tried to pinpoint the source. As did Erina. It would have been easier if it didn't stop and start at irregular intervals. It managed to be both close and afar at the same time. A little like how she imagined it'd be hearing something through a fish tank would be. A very large fish tank.

'Please tell me you heard that?' Erina beseeched her companion.

'That one?' Sam asked, cocking his head to the side. His ears were as much on alert as they could be. Had he been a dog they'd have been standing straight up and pointy. 'I heard it, yes.'

'Where is it coming from? Can you tell?'

Sam considered the question for a while. 'I do believe it's coming from below the ground,' he said, eventually.

'Whatever it is, it seems to be moving away,' Erina said, eyeing the ground beneath her feet suspiciously. The hill *looked* innocent enough. She'd ridden here many times. That didn't have to mean *anything*. Things … changed.

'They're fading, certainly,' Sam agreed.

The two of them exchanged a glance, their expressions almost perfect mirrors of each other.

'You don't think…' Erina began.

'The chambers we found aren't the only underground spaces here,' Sam finished.

'How far do you think it extends?'

'Might not all be the same cave system,' Sam said. 'Most likely isn't.'

'But what if it is?' Erina asked.

It made sense. There were caves (of the ordinary type) in the Valley. Of course there were. Caves were a perfectly natural part of the geography … and geology. They sort of came with the whole "planet" thing. Heck, you even found caves on asteroids. Or *in* them, at least.

Erina made a face. Natural it might be, but that didn't mean she'd expected to find it below her feet *out here*. Of course, she hadn't expected to find it below her living room, either.

'Just one surprise after another,' she sighed. 'Come on. Might as well get this over with.'

It looked so serene up here (minus the boulders having come loose in the last storm and making their own, now very flat, road through the forest before coming to rest in a combination of twisted trees that non-the-less remained upright). The forest had won in the end.

Who knew what was hiding down below? *Who* was hiding down below?

There couldn't be other people here, could there? *Something* had to be making that sound.

Erina groaned. 'Oh gosh, I do hope it's not zombies,' she said.

'You've been watching too many holos, My Lady.'

Erina huffed. 'If this place has taught me anything, it's not to rule out anything. Mushroom induced shuffling madness or something is still zombies in my book.'

'You just made that up,' Sam accused her, physically restraining one hand from facepalming with the other.

Erina grinned. He wasn't wrong there. 'Maaybee…' she said.

Sam, meanwhile, gave the whole idea some serious thought, despite how casually he'd dismissed it out loud. It was true that she'd lived here much longer than he had and was, presumably, more familiar with the location. That didn't mean she knew everything there was to know about the place. She'd been very upfront about that before he even signed the contract.

He'd done his best to familiarize himself as much as possible in the, relatively, short time since he'd arrived. There was so much *he* didn't know, but he did take extra care not to do things that Erina specified he should never, ever, do. She'd demonstrated on his very first day just how treacherous — and dangerous — doing even innocuous things could be if you applied planetary logic to this place.

Also, there *had* been some *very* unusual clauses in that employment contract, so it wasn't that he hadn't been forewarned. And that wasn't counting the, quite frankly, peculiar and mysterious way he and Wave Rock had arrived in the first place.

That had been one bizarre journey, yet not half as strange as the fact he'd still not been able to find the way back. Not through that route. From this side it might as well not even exist anymore.

He'd been up that way several times by now, and on neither occasion had he found even a single trace of that it had ever been there in the first place. Indeed, part of what he'd taken as a passageway was now solid mountain.

Not to mention that none of those things even began accounting for how "here" existed in the first place.

This could well just be another, unexplained, mystery that would remain just that. A mystery. This entire solar system had plenty of those. A good thing he wasn't prone to anxiety, Sam thought. This place could get under your skin, if you let down your guard.

He *still* didn't think it was zombies.

'The sound appears to have disappeared,' Sam pointed out.

'So it has,' Erina agreed, after straining to try to pick up even the remnants of it. 'Your ears are better than mine. I'll take your word for it.'

A BALANCING ACT

In the coming days, and then weeks, the strange sound didn't stay gone. But it didn't exactly stay around, either. Though if it was the *same* sound or even the same thing causing it was anyone's guess.

By now they didn't only catch it out in the wilds. Soon enough they'd both started to hear it not just from below the new paddock, but out in the fields*. Erina swore one time she'd heard it out in the Dead Forest. They'd even caught it on a journey out to the deep lakes, and that was *not* a short journey away.

At that point the only thing that kept Erina from going after whatever it was, was the fact that there was quite a bit of rock between her and it. Not solid rock, she guessed, though that was exactly that, just a guess. The cause of the sound *could* be a giant worm burrowing through the bedrock for all she knew — though the clip clop echo suggested it wasn't.

It seemed every day their theories as to what it could be became more and more outlandish.

'Maybe we have some sort of underground caterpillar with a fetish for wearing shoes on their hands?' Erina suggested, waving her own hand over the dusty summer ground. 'Feet? You know what I mean.'

'You're not planning on trying to dig through that, are you, My Lady?' Sam asked as Erina stared intently at the dirt next to the paddock.

* Well, from *below* the fields, technically speaking.

Neither of the horses were, by now, paying any attention. Their only interest was in the buckets of feed their humans had brought earlier.

That suggested it wasn't something *that* scary, didn't it?

Erina snorted. 'It's not like we can order a mobile borer with a pulse drill and aim it at the ground the next time this *thing* shows up again,' she said. 'The dratted thing wouldn't work. Not until they find a better power-source.'

'Different, not better,' Sam corrected. 'But yes, I am aware, My Lady.' Considering the intensity gleaming in her eyes, Seranthiem was relieved that Erina wasn't already trying to claw away at the ground with her bare hands, clods of earth and grass flying in all directions.

The soil would be an inconvenience to dig through. The rock beneath that would be impossible. With your hands, that was. Which was, Sam was led to believe, the only reason she hadn't already tried.

Even then, whatever was making that sound probably was able to move faster than she'd be able to dig.

'AH! This is driving me *nuts*!' Erina swore, walking in circles, and pulling at her hair in frustration.

Yet it kept continuing. If anything, as the days went on by it seemed to happen more and more frequently.

'Is it just me or is this thing *following* us?' Erina asked while helping giving Wave Rock a wash in the stable yard. She stared angrily into the distance after catching just a hint of sound before it, once more, faded away. 'It was out by the hayfields only yesterday.'

'I can certainly agree that it feels that way,' Sam nodded thoughtfully, dunking a green sponge into a bucket of water. 'Normally I would say it's unlikely but not impossible. Might not even be the same creature. If it is a creature at all. Could simply be a geological disturbance … of some sort.'

It sounded farfetched even as the words left his mouth. Sam tried to remember if planets were supposed to do that sort of thing. Geology was not his area of expertise.

Erina made a face.

'Please, don't let it be a giant, underground, tentacle monster.'

Sam tried very hard not to roll his eyes *or* laugh. He must have not been as successful as he'd hoped, for Erina gave him one of her side-eyes.

‘What? It *could* be.’

‘It’s most likely a natural phenomenon,’ Sam said. He didn’t actually believe that, he just felt morally obligated to provide some sort of opposition on the matter.

‘Or ants. Ants are natural. *Giant*, carnivorous, ants. And we’re just living on top of a gigantic anthill.’

‘Now you’re being ridiculous, My Lady,’ Sam admonished. And doing it on purpose, I’m sure of it.

He didn’t say that last part out loud.

Erina stuck her tongue out at him, before turning serious once more. ‘My *brain* knows that,’ she confessed. ‘My self-preservation is not convinced.’

❋❋❋

‘Step, Wave!’

Sam’s voice was barely a whisper, yet he’d not more than uttered those words before the dun coloured horse took a single step sideways and stopped. Now each hoof rested on a different stone than before.

‘Good boy,’ Sam praised him. ‘Step.’

Once more Wave Rock moved sideways, listening intently to the directions from both voice and gestures. He had no wish to end up in the water. He’d seen the things that swam around down there. They might be small, but they were the opposite of friendly.

The stone “bridge” was not the way he’d have preferred to cross this particular stretch of water, however. A sensible horse would have gone around the lakeshore, he thought.

The flat stones might barely be above the lake’s surface, but they were more pillars than they were the flat stones you might find in a river. In fact, they might actually have been pillars at some point. Some had shifted position as the sandy bottom had. Others had fallen away, lying cracked and broken under layers and layers of sediment.

You could sort of skip across them from one side of the lake to the other, if you were really careful, as long as you went slowly and didn’t shift their, or your, balance too much.

'Good work, Wave.' Sam patted his horse's muscular neck.

'Well, that was one way to do it,' Erina commented as the pair reached the far shore on the other side of Fairy Lake. She realized she'd been holding her breath the whole time.

She'd crossed that herself, but never on horseback. She didn't think she'd want to unless really, really, desperate. Sam didn't seem to have any such concern.

'Good thing you and I just went the long away around, right boy?' She leaned forward and patted Harlan on the neck, ruffling bits of his mane at the base.

'See, there was no reason for concern.' Sam tilted his head slightly, some of the long, silver, locks falling across his shoulder.

Erina merely she shook her head.

'Only for you Sam. Only for you.' She patted Harlan again. 'You have to admire him,' she said to the trias. 'You really do. Most people wouldn't even *imagine* trying to ride across the Singing Rocks.'

Aside from sometimes being *under* the water, the collection of "rocks" was sparse and depending on which course you took across them, you might be left with a dead end, i.e. stuck with one foot on several rocks and no way to turn around and every other stone too far away.

She'd never thought of using them as a pathway when *riding*.

It had saved a lot of time. No argument there. She'd expected having at least an hour or more to herself.

Wave nickering upon seeing his friends again, having been parted from them a whole morning.

'We were only away for a few hours,' Erina mumbled at him, but the dun didn't seem to take that to heart.

Continuing on, they eventually stopped to rest by one of the numerous much smaller bodies of water that bordered Fairy Lake. On a map some might have been referred to as little more than ponds (though she'd seen some pretty big things labelled "ponds" on Soulcatcher and there was no way anyone was going to call them oceans no matter how vast they were when not even one was even deep enough to wet your ankles), but they certainly were intimate sized, so to speak.

As most of its kind here, this one was being fed by tiny, trickling, streams that crisscrossed the landscape — sometimes so small and unobtrusive that you didn't know they were even there until you stepped in them and your socks got soaked. Occasionally one would vanish only to reappear, the same stream, several hundred meters (and possibly a hill or rocky crevasse) later. While some made sense — and had perfectly natural, logical, reasons for doing what they did — there were also those that simply vanished in thin air in one place and reappeared, just as abruptly, a few meters downstream – as if someone had taken a large eraser to the visual stream but the background water physics were still there.

Water, mostly, but not always, stayed where it was expected to … in the ground. At least it did so when it knew you were watching.

'What did you expect from a place with an up-and-down stream?' Erina asked herself. 'Don't expect things to start making sense now.'

'It does appear that has never stopped them before,' Sam agreed. 'Also, didn't you say this used to be *on the other side of the forest*?'

'I did, didn't I?' Erina narrowed her eyes suspiciously. Turning this way then that, they didn't seem to have wandered off and gotten lost themselves. That didn't leave a lot of alternatives…

For that matter, where *did* all the water actually come from? If it all came from snowmelt up in the mountains, with the amount of rain and snow they got each year even Snowfell should have been a grey rock millennia ago. It certainly shouldn't be a white cone draped in the feint veil of gossamer.

A fact that Sam had already commented on that had brought on this whole conversation, and visit, to begin with. How could she explain something when she didn't understand it herself? Showing him took so much less time and effort and, as a bonus, he could now join in the general state of confounded conundrum that plagued most days when you started to actually think about it.

'It can't be the rain,' Erina mused. 'There's no way the catchment area is big enough for all these streams to collect that much water continuously.'

That was the second part of the mystery. Or third, she'd lost count. If some of them had dried up during the summer, that'd balance out … a bit. But the only time something here dried up was if something, like a rockfall or a sleeping kelpie, blocked their source, and then that water would just go somewhere else.

Also, there was a lot of water running through the Valley. If it had all been draining onto the valley floor the whole place should have turned into one big lake at this point, she was sure of it.

Erina dipped her canteen in the bubbling brook that fed this particular tiny body of water not bothering to get out of the saddle to do so. Harlan didn't bother. He preferred water that didn't try to escape and fizzled in nostrils and stuck his muzzle into the pond instead.

'Three days out here … hunting these "mysterious" sounds and we're still no wiser.' Erina leaned forwards in her saddle, both her hands pressing down on the pommel.

'At least this time they've been consistent enough we have been able to follow them,' Seranthiem pointed out.

To Sam's ears she sounded annoyed. Though he didn't care to guess if it was because they hadn't found the source of said mystery or due to them being dragged all the way out here on a, in his eyes, wild rach chase in the first place.

It had started as him merely expressing an interest in understanding the Valley better. Erina deciding to show him one of the more … distinct … examples and now, being here, having it all overshadowed by the hounding of goodness knew what.

He, at least, hoped it was hounding them. Haunting them was a great deal more concerning … and he'd have no idea how to deal with that. He was sure ghosts weren't real but at this point he was starting to wonder if someone had told the ghosts that?

Not thirty minutes later what had been a laid-back jaunt had morphed into a high speed chase. Whatever it was down there, it had taken off.

'Something must have spooked it,' Erina shouted over the rhythmic thuds of the horses' hooves. 'It's never gone this fast before.'

'It's a lot easier to follow now,' Sam called back.

This was true. Not only were the sounds louder but they were more consistent, too. Though they still couldn't quite make out *what* they were. The transfer through the earth and soil and rock distorted and dulled everything. But they could follow it. And follow it they did.

Then, suddenly, it stopped. The two riders and horses milled about on the surface. The horses were snorting and stomping, excited by the chase. The riders were trying to get their bearings and ending up with nothing.

'There it is again!'

'After it! It's getting fainter!'

'That way,' Sam pointed as Wave Rock whirled around, taking off once more.

Erina let out a shout and nudged her own mount forward. Harlan, already impatient with restless legs, fell into a staccato trot for but a few steps before settling down into something a little more suitable for the sparse woodland and underbrush they were currently riding through.

Excited or not, no reason to put his hooves through a clump of moss only to find it was three meters deep. A good way to break a leg. He wasn't doing that again. Breaking a neck would be a bit more … permanent. Nope. Not doing that.

Still, he tossed his head, sending the black and white mane flying, and whinnied. His ears swivelled around. He, too, was catching the occasionally dull echo of hoof steps from below the ground. He'd heard it many times.

He'd never chased after it before.

This was fun.

Seranthiem drew to a halt. If his eyes wasn't mistaken… Yes. Finally. A real clue. He turned in the saddle, catching his companion's attention as Erina drew up next to him.

'My Lady.'

'Yes, Sam?'

'I think I've found something,' Sam said.

And so he had.

It wasn't so much a path as it was a trail. It didn't even qualify as a game trail, used by multiple critters. It was too faint for that. Or maybe it was just old? But then why wasn't it more overgrown?

'*Something* is coming and going,' Erina said. 'Not very often, by the looks of things.'

‘That is precisely what’s worrying me,’ Sam replied. ‘It would seem this subterranean entity isn’t actually confined to the undergrounds.’

He was scanning their surroundings for anything that might be hiding in the bushes. Might *be* the bushes.

Erina seemed far more laid back about this than he’d expected. Considering she’d taken to wearing the black garment they’d found under the house, that, right now, gave her the appearance of a very nonchalant crow. One that was satisfied waiting you out.

Not that she usually appeared worried or concerned out here, Sam reminded himself.

In contrast, he certainly didn’t care for their current location. The forest here had grown quite thick, but the underbrush was less leafy — so much the pendulum has swung to the entirely opposite end. There were extra spikes on *everything*. Leaning forwards, he was worried about Wave Rock’s legs.

Harlan didn’t seem to care, but Erina, herself, could already count several tears in the packs they’d brought with them.

‘I hate to say it,’ Erina said, ‘but we better slow down. You want to take the lead?’

Single file seemed sensible. Whatever had created this trail, it clearly wasn’t very wide. Things kept scraping against her legs. If they pushed the horses into a run here, they’d be more likely to get flaked off like dried coconuts on a week old cake.

‘Any critters living out this way better have a thick hide,’ she muttered, pulling another thorny twig out of her hair. How had that gotten in there?

‘I suggest we dismount and *walk* the horses,’ Sam said.

So they did just that.

Harlan tried to dig his head under an arm brimming with cloth. Seeing how short Erina was, this was quite the feat. If he’d been a dog he would have wined. This had gone from exciting to … something else … very fast.

Planting all four hooves on the mossy forest floor the stallion refused to budge.

In Sam’s eyes, this made him the most sensible out of the four of them. He wished he could do the same … but that would be silly.

Of course, s*ensible* people didn’t hear enigmatic sounds in the darkness of the night and *went outside* to investigate. By this point he'd come to terms with that *sensible* wasn't a word anyone who knew Erina would use to describe her. There was a frown currently lodged in her forehead that suggested she'd gotten to the point where she was as likely to let things be as a rach was to let go of a half-dead chicken.

But then Cognitors tended to need to be very out-of-the-box kind of people to begin with. It was just that their usual *modus operandi* involved talking. Negotiations. He simply couldn't see Erina doing that.

By now he'd gotten the impression that in her old job, Erina's position had been less straight forward than her old title suggested.

Reckless, that's what the word he was looking for was. Though, he had to give her that while she seemed perfectly happy to throw her own wellbeing out the window* this didn't extend to doing so with everyone else's.

He was grateful for that. If she'd turned out to be the type to play with other people's lives, he'd have left almost as soon as he'd arrived — even if that had meant he'd needed to live out in the wilds until the next opportunity to actually leave the Valley presented itself.

He might have called her "plucky" but since he didn't relish having his face peeled off and roasted he'd never done so. Not out loud. And certainly not to her face.

Sure, she might look like a light breeze would make her topple over, but by now he knew just how deceptive that was. Not many people he'd ever known were able to go from whimsical to lethal in less time it took your heart to beat once … and then go right back to talking about the weather as if nothing had happened, blood dripping from their hair.

Not *their* blood, he hastened to clarify to himself. Sam studied the image he'd been creating in his mind then shook his head. No, that was *too* cartoonish.

Still, he pitied the creature they were chasing should it turn on them. For all her complaining, making it sound as if she'd run away the moment one showed up, it would be a foolish something that would try to make a meal out of his employer.

Now, he would have appreciated it even more if he hadn't been made to

* Or off a cliff, through a black hole, or whatever else came by to say hello.

tag along on some of these little excursions like the one they were currently on and said beasties wouldn't have the opportunity to make a meal out of *him*.

Sam tried taking a deep breath. It only half worked at making him feel any better. But what else could he do? Turn around and go home? Leave the intrepid explorer to go into the dark all on their own?

Even if Erina would have been fine with that, he wasn't.

'I'll move ahead,' he said.

Sam's voice was barely a whisper. Not because they'd seen anything yet but the forest around them was eerily silent.

It had been … for a while now. If anything, the only sounds were the ones they brought with them. Oh, and buzzing. A myriad of little crawling, flying, things were busy doing their own thing. That included eating them. Sam swatted at an enterprising mosquito that had landed on his nose.

Somehow he didn't think what they were looking for would be found in a giant hive.

The idea didn't appeal, either. He shook that thought off while handing over Rocky's reins to Erina. Neither of them were keen on going this way but it *was* the direction the last sound they'd caught and, judging from the way the rocky terrain beginning to reveal itself rising out of the forest floor promised having to go around the entire area if what they were looking for happened to be on the other side, well…

Currently he was betting on that whatever they were chasing would also have had to go around, and that would have, probably, made sounds in a different direction. Their own little party was hardly quiet, after all. Ergo, they went straight ahead.

Normally he tried to gather more information before making any such rash decisions, but they'd been out here long enough. Right now all he wanted to was to go back home.

Part of him was thinking that he'd have done much better on his own. Alone he could move silently … almost soundlessly, even. When he wanted to.

As it turned out, Seranthiem wasn't the only pretend shadow stalking through this section of the forest.

Although the second one wasn't exactly moving, except back and forth.

Nervously. Restlessly. A black shadow against mossy stone. The forest parted way and grew around, and on top of, a chunk of land pressed up above itself.

Sam quietly slipped behind a thick, grey, tree trunk. They'd found their target at last.

Still partially concealed by all the vegetation, a dark body moved in and out of view. There was only one reasonable explanation, Sam thought. It must be lurking near the mouth of a cave.

Was that how it got around? It made sense there had to be entry points to the world below, but he hadn't expected to find one here. Sam lowered himself towards the forest floor, keeping out of sight. One step closer. Another.

Somewhere way behind him Harlan snorted, loudly. The shadow threw its head up, an unnerving screech erupting from its throat. It whirled around and, to a strong echo of hooves upon stone, disappeared into the earth's interior.

'What was that?' his companion asked as she caught up, able to find the room up here, right next to the mouth of the cave.

'Wait, it did what?' she asked, as Sam gave her a brief run-down on what had just happened.

He pointed towards where the shadow had disappeared. 'That way,' he said.

Erina stared at it. It was hardly what you'd call accessible. Not terribly inviting, either. And at any other angle other than straight ahead it looked more like a gap between a mountain troll's teeth, if they'd fallen on their side and been lost to nature.

It was all the moss, Sam decided. It was playing tricks even on his imagination.

Checking his footing, the entire area immediately around this place seemed damper than the forest they'd come up through. Some had collected into tiny pools of mud where the trail had been beaten down. The bushes and vines pushed aside … repeatedly.

'Did you get a good look at it?' Erina wondered, but Sam shook his head.

'It kept fading in and out of the shadow, but I would say it's about the size of a horse.'

'That doesn't actually say much, you know. And that didn't sound like any horse I know,' Erina said. 'But I'll take your word for it.'

Sam gingerly touched the stone with his bare hand. 'Cold,' he reported.

'And you're *sure* this not-quite-a-horse went in here?'

'Yes.'

'And you're sure it's what's been making all this noise? It wasn't just a half-starved red beaver or something?'

'Positive.'

'Wonderful.' Erina took a deep breath. 'Oh well, only one way to find out I expect. You did say you thought we needed more horses.'

'Wait, I didn't say... You don't even know if it's...' Sam stopped for breath, mocked by his heart thrumming at a different gear than normal. 'Please tell me you're not serious!' he begged.

From Erina that would have been a sarcastic remark followed by a grimace. From Sam it was more of a desperate pleading sprinkled with disbelief. A lot of disbelief.

'Come now, Sam. Live a little, why don't you?' Erina poked her companion in the shoulder with a finger. 'You only live once.'

'It's precisely because I wish to stay that way that I think this is a bad idea,' Sam muttered lightly under his breath.

'What was that?'

'Nothing, My Lady.'

'Good.'

Sam tried to school his face back to normalcy, reaching for the mask of serenity and finding only the mask of barely contained despair and utter capitulation. Truth was this was hardly the craziest* thing he'd been asked to partake in since arriving at High Fyelds.

It wasn't even the most dangerous thing he'd done *on his own*. None of the others had, however, been for such … frivolous … reasons. He tried to hold back a shudder.

With a sinking heart he realized that if his life in the Valley so far was any indicator, it wasn't likely to *stay* in the top ten.

Even so, the cave mouth was hardly the most inviting entryway he'd ever prepared to walk, run, sail, swim, or otherwise move, through. Voluntarily or otherwise.

* AKA most "dangerous".

'Don't worry, Sam. I don't think we need to worry about drowning,' Erina said, noticing his distain when examining the water pooling around the loose rocks nearby.

'Hmm?'

'Going by the amount it rains, the Valley should have run out a long time ago if that was the case. Either that, or there was a lot more stored underground that, somehow, made its way up here.' Erina continued.

'That's not what I was worried about,' Sam admitted. He nodded towards the two horses now standing placidly behind them.

'No way I'm leaving them behind.' Erina crossed her arms, challenging her companion. 'I know what hides in these woods.'

'Very well,' Sam said.

She *was* the boss, technically and legally speaking. If anything did happen, it would be her responsibility.

Even so… He considered the options for a moment. Did he have any *actual* good reasons not to do this? It was, he thought, foolish. But it would hardly be the most foolish thing he'd ever done.

As it was, it was slowly and carefully that they made their way down into the subterranean world. All four of them. Eventually.

Wave Rocky followed Sam in without question. Convincing Harlan to come along had turned out to be a lot harder. Underground wasn't a place he had very good memories of.

'How deep do you think this goes?' Erina asked Sam after less than half-an-hour.

He suspected it was more of a rhetorical question. She did have a habit of talking to herself.

'I don't know,' Sam replied, settling for blunt honesty. 'It's not steep, so if it continues at the same incline, I would say … not very. As it is, it's already changing structure from where we entered.'

'That it is,' Erina nodded. 'The floor is suspiciously smooth, isn't it? For a cave system.'

Sam agreed with that. Aside from the cave itself — well, caverns, really at this point — the path, for it could hardly be called anything else, was cleared of such things as shallow rock pools* and inconvenient, half eroded, rock formations.

It had started to smell musty once they'd entered the dark world, but now the air in their nostrils was clean, clear, and cold.

It took passing through several more small caverns before the things they both expected to find, such as the stalagmites and stalactites, began to appear. At one point one set of caverns were filled with them, like a rocky cathedral built out of runny candles only of water and stone. Layer upon layer covering the walls and ceiling and most of the floor.

The entire experience was becoming more like an actual subterranean exploration than a quick jaunt into the underground. At least there hadn't been anything down here that moved, other than shadows dancing through the hallways, forming weird and wonderful shapes as their lights shifted and moved as they walked.

If the horses spooked down here they'd be in a lot of trouble. Yet they appeared no closer to their quarry.

Occasionally there was a small "tink" as some water droplet somewhere lost its battle with gravity.

'Considering what I know of the Valley, I had expected to come across at least one giant chasm by now,' Sam mused. 'Wonder why we haven't?'

'Same reason we didn't run into any giant water bears I expect,' Erina quipped. 'Heard they're pretty much indestructible. This looks like a good place for things like that.'

'You told me the Valley doesn't have bears,' Sam said, accusingly.

'That's not... Ah, forget it,' Erina waved away the entire conversation. 'Let's just focus on getting through this cave, shall we? I think I spotted another opening up ahead. Move the light a bit, will you?'

'A large subterranean predator seems unlikely,' Sam said, unwilling to drop the topic just like that.

'Stranger things have happened,' Erina replied, rolling her eyes. 'Lots and lots of small ones don't exactly fill me with glee, either. In fact, that's' probably even worse. Thanks.'

'Your imagination is working overdrive ... *again* ... My Lady.'

* Where a gazillion of cave shrimp civilizations strived for enlightenment.

'Nope,' Erina shot back. 'My imagination hasn't even started yet.'

❊❊❊

'Dark, dank, and decrepit!' Erina made a disgusted sound in the back of her throat.

Behind them, they still towed both their mounts who, by now, were starting to wonder if their favourite two-legs were going to argue all the way to … wherever they were going.

Judging by how they'd been chattering back and forth for the last hour, it sure seemed that way. Harlan snorted, his companion giving him a quick, friendly nibble, as if telling him not to worry so much.

Neither Sam nor Erina would, probably, have cared to know they were being judged at the moment, so it was a good thing they didn't know.

'Don't you just love it down here?' Erina complained. She eyed up the wonders, what little their light lit up, and made a face. 'Tell me, do you bring all the girls here?'

Seranthiem's own face didn't as much as twitch. He was learning to tell when to take Erina seriously and right now was certainly not it.

'It's not that bad,' Sam insisted. 'And not that dark, either. For being underground, I mean. Remember all those glow-worms on the ceiling of the last cavern?'

'I'm trying very hard not to,' Erina said. 'Bleh.'

Enclosed spaces weren't exactly her favourite at the best of times*. At least the caverns, crawlspaces, and tunnels had, so far, not been small enough to feel truly claustrophobic, as long as she remembered not to think about them.

Which was really hard when you were walking right inside them.

'Ridiculous', Erina muttered to herself. She had no problem with cramped space when *in* space. A standard cockpit was hardly luxurious in terms of room and while yes, while her own ship had done away with "cramped" in general, that was because she liked being comfortable, not because she turned into a blubbering wreck when it wasn't available.

* One of the reasons her old "personal" ship had been more than a cockpit and a pair of engines despite, technically, being a one-pilot-fighter. She liked being able to actually move more than three centimetres to either side. She had been especially fond of the pantry.

Even so, while some of the caverns here — especially one they'd only been able to view from above through an opening in one of the tunnel walls — were the size of a small cathedral, most of them weren't. Though even the smallest actual cavern would have fit a decent sized house they didn't feel that big. They crept up on you, in the dark. When you turned away, how did you know they weren't right there, a hair's breadth behind you?

You didn't. By now the cold sweat on her back had soaked through her shirt.

Occasionally they'd walk past something that suggested there had, once, been a thriving ecosystem down here. Curious stains of colour. Patterns woven into the rock as if by waving carpets clinging to the wall. Peculiar shaped indentations in the stone that had once been alive. Large, fossilized things that might have been some form of mushroom … once. That one had required a detour.

The most infuriating of all, was that they kept hearing their quarry … just a little bit further away than where they were. Like them it was constantly moving. Like them, it wasn't moving very fast.

They even passed by gatherings of the tiniest crystal clusters imaginable. Mostly small ones, little more than a glimmer in the dark when their light flashed over them. Pretty, but other than that they didn't think about them*.

'How unfortunate *they* don't glow,' Erina had griped. 'Put that in a lantern and we'd have all the light we'd need.'

'They're a bit small.'

'Good point. Let's not do that then.'

As they moved on there were plenty of broken, jagged, rocks that had, at some point in the past, toppled over and, in parts, filled the floor down here with stone dust, enough of it to make them cough and try not to stir any more of it up.

She could do without tripping over anything else at this point. The floor down here was hardy even. Whatever had made *that* had obviously not come down this deep. It took time and care to guide the horses. The last thing they needed was to get stuck down here.

Getting impaled on a rock spire was undoubtedly as unpleasant as getting

* Things might have gone very differently if they had… Or, at least, faster.

impaled on anything else.

How many bruises had this little "adventure" left her with already? Erina wasn't looking forward to finding out once she was back at the stables. She was beginning to have second thoughts about this whole thing.

At least the worst Harlan had gotten were burrs and twigs in his mane and tail.

Maybe he was a lot better suited for this? After all, unlike her, he was from the Valley. She'd only ended up here by accident. Literally.

Maybe that was why he was also the first to catch sight of their quarry? Harlan rolled bright blue eyes, tossed his head up and let out a loud harrumph and a whinny that, down here, rolled off the stony walls and just kept on going.

They caught a glimpse of something moving up ahead. Just a quick glint of a teal glow. Pinpricks of light in the dark. Two of them.

Sam swung the light cone around. For a second it reflected off a shiny, lithe, body, as if it had struck an oil slick. Then, an echo of clappering hooves on rock rained down on them as, startled into a run, the shadow disappeared into yet another gallery.

'Finally!' Erina exclaimed. 'Whoah! Whoah! Easy there, Harlan!'

The trias jigged in place. 'Did you see that?' Erina asked, keeping a light hand on the reins, letting him get it out of his system.

'I did,' Sam acknowledged. Part of him wanted to jump on Wave Rock's back and go after their fleeing target. But going anywhere down here fast was a recipe for disaster even if you already knew your way around. Never mind if you didn't.

'What are we standing here for then? After it!'

Every chaser's instinct screamed at them to run, to pounce. Every ounce of common sense did the exact opposite … only less loudly. They compromised by, unanimously, moving forward at a brisk jog.

The echoes down here were treacherous. You could take the most ordinary sound and two reverberations later it'd have turned into something trying to creep up your back.

As such, when the shadow they were chasing dashed into yet another gallery, its pursuers too close, too scary, it proved to be the wrong one. As a cave it wasn't a bad one. If anyone had had time to stop to admire it, it was actually very well adorned. It did, however, have one rather important flaw.

There was no way out. Well, other than the same way he'd come in. It was therefore rather unfortunate that there were now four unsolicited tails between him and it.

A *slight* miscalculation on his part.

What was supposed to have been one of the more direct exits to the surface world, featuring a mostly empty long tunnel, had turned out to be a dead end. He'd taken the wrong turn.

The sharp, staccato, click-clack that the pursuers had been following became broken and irregular. Frantic. Snorts, screeches, even a whinny, rang through the stone halls.

Seranthiem and Erina exchanged a glance.

'That sounded like a horse,' Sam said.

'Some of it did,' Erina replied. 'And here I thought we'd been tracking a predator.'

'What is *a horse* doing down here?'

'I don't know. Why *is* a horse running around in the dark?'

The one opening to the cave wasn't very wide and, with the four of them, they effectively blocked it. The mystery horse might try to shove his way through, but there was no way he'd be able to dash right past them.

With the sounds now coming from the far end, there was no need to search. Sam swung the light around, pointing it straight at the source.

Running back and forth up against the far wall the black shadow they'd been chasing tried to get away … through the wall of stone. Frantic, froth now covered his entire chest.

He had to get away. To get out. Everything was close. Everyone was too close. What was going on? Away. Away!

'Easy there now, we're not going to hurt you!' Sam hummed softly.

'I don't think he believes you,' Erina said.

Sam wasn't going to argue with that. The animal clearly didn't want to be there. Outmatched in numbers on one side and thoroughly defeated by a rock on the other, the horse wasn't going to get through that side in a hurry. Not unless he could burrow through the ground — and if so, why hadn't he done that already?

Of course, then it would definitely not have been a horse they'd been chasing all this time.

Wave Rock was unperturbed. Not that Erina was surprised. The impression she'd gotten of him was that he shared more than his name with his namesake. He was, if you wanted to be corny about it, "steady as a rock".

She'd never asked why Seranthiem had named him that. For some reason, now she was curious. How peculiar. Erina resigned herself to that she'd have to get around to asking … at some point.

In comparison, Harlan was alert. Not nervous, per se, though certainly not comfortable with their current situation.

The contrast to the cornered, black, horse couldn't be bigger.

'Calm down… It's okay… Calm…'

Soothing words was not having much of an effect, or any effect at all. If anything it seemed to rile the horse up even more.

Sam was right about them not being understood. Why would they be? Strange creatures from the world above that they must be in his eyes.

It was, in the end, less a question of capturing their erstwhile quarry and more of an exhausted surrender on his part. It wasn't as if he'd had a lot of energy left to begin with.

Mind you, that wasn't the only reason why he'd needed to move at less than breakneck speed through these caverns. He almost never went fast anywhere. If he wasn't careful he'd end up tripping over himself. His mane and tail draped along the floor, snagging in anything it could.

'You did say you thought we should get another horse,' Erina pointed out.

'I would call him more *equine adjacent*,' Sam insisted.

The inconvenient mane and tail hadn't been their only surprise. The teal glowing eyes was another. Yet nowhere near as startling as the five horns adorning the slender head.

They made sure to keep their distance from those.

The climb back up to the surface was a lot quicker than the descent. Not because they knew the way back, but because the path that the black horse hadn't taken turned out to, after Sam took a peek a little further ahead, to have faint traces of sunlight.

Heading up that tunnel it didn't even take twenty minutes before they could see blue. Finding themselves once more under a brighter sky, they took a moment to just breathe in the air, the scents of the world above. No longer in fear of hitting their heads on the ceiling, it felt like a weight was falling off their shoulders.

'We could just release him right here,' Sam said as they exited the cave mouth.

'And what good would that do?' Erina asked, noting that Sam hadn't sounded very comfortable with the idea himself. 'Look at him, he's two sandwiches away from starving. Hardly more than skin and bone.'

It wasn't *quite* that bad, Sam thought. But, he had to admit that Erina had a point. The black shadow was less lithe than he was gaunt.

Why, he wasn't sure. The Valley had plenty of food, especially at this time of the year. It was a veritable cornucopia. It wasn't like the horse needed to hunt down the grass and kill it.

Though, underground *was* different. What ecosystem he'd seen traces of down there had been mostly long gone or very, very rudimentary.

But, then, the horse had hardly been trapped down there, had he? They'd chased him *into* the subterranean world, not flushed him out of it.

Though, he still wasn't entirely comfortable calling him a horse. He'd worked with horses and nightmares long enough, sometimes the difference was small, but it was always there.

If he compared him to Harlan, there was the same proud arch to the neck. A similar slenderness to the delicate head — though that was where *that* similarity ended, the two heads weren't remotely the same shape. A longer, but also thin, body with similarly thin legs for all that the amount of them were clearly distributed differently.

It was only when you took in all the attributes at the same time that you realized that the proportions were all wonky … and why your brain had been insisting that something was wrong.

He had the shape of something that had been made by someone that had had a horse described to them by someone who really liked horses but didn't actually know very much about them.

BITE ME (NOT)

‘He looks small,’ Sam said.

‘He’s taller than Harlan,’ Erina pointed out. ‘But more slender. Didn’t think that was possible. Scrawnier, too.’

‘That is obvious.’

They were standing by the paddock. The black “horse” was huddling on the other side, as far away from them as possible.

‘If you didn’t insist that nothing enters the Valley, I would have assumed him to be an escaped nightmare,’ Sam said.

‘I can understand why. Still, he seems mostly horse-ish to me.’

That did seem to be the case. Though, seeing how most nightmares had the base anatomy and genome of equines, this wasn’t really and end-all-arguments statement.

Both mane and tail were long. Ridiculously long. They were both draping on the ground. Any time he’d move, they’d drag behind him. Slowing him down. Threatening to send him stumbling to his knees.

They were also very, very tangled. No surprise there.

‘I’m amazed he managed to move through all that woodland,’ Erina said. ‘Poor thing.’

The tail was the worst. A tangled mess coiled on the ground like a very confused mess of black and red snakes. But his coat didn’t look that great, either. Though even in this state it was clear that black and red was a general theme when it came to end-points — whether they were talking about hair, legs, or the tips of some very pointed horns.

All five of them.

As if there needed to be another dead giveaway that the newest arrival wasn't an ordinary horse.

'But not a unicorn,' Erina commented.

'Obviously,' Sam agreed. 'Too many horns.'

Not only were there five of them (which had to be heavy, Erina thought) they were shaped like thick scimitars. As they'd already discovered, the things were scarily sharp not just at the tip but all along the thin edge, as if, indeed, they'd been meant to slice things open. Running from above his forehead all the way down to the nose-back, they appeared to form a solid frame at the base, though decreasing in size as you went downwards.

On someone else, they probably would have looked quite intimidating.

'I hope he doesn't pick up any bad habits from Harlan,' Erina said, thinking that having that head trying to nuzzle under her arm would be unpleasant. 'Might as well just stick me in a meat slicer. Who knows, I could make a good salami.'

'A five pronged kebab is more likely,' Sam said.

'Thanks.' Erina shot her companion a silent glare. One he took in stride.

'Unusual red colour,' Sam continued.

This was also true. While Harlan, as a trias, had red as one of his three coat colours, it was generally a cheery sort of bright red. Here, in the sunlight, what had appeared to be an entirely black coat wrapped in midnight, was actually accented by a blend of black and a deep, dark, red running towards all the points and tips. The legs. The mane. The tail. Even the horns looked as if blood had been dripping from them, then been frozen in place.

The "wading through rivers of blood" theme was playing in the back of both their minds. Something that wasn't offset in the least by the eyes, which weren't the depths of pitch and despair, but a sort of spooky pale blue teal.

Harlan, too, had blue eyes. That was where the similarities ended. Not only were these completely lacking in an iris, whites, or anything else. There was also the small fact that they glowed.

Up here, in daylight, they looked a little like faint fireflies that had stayed out too long the next morning. Down in the world of the caves below they had been burning embers of fire. Blue fire.

'This is going to take a lot of work,' Sam said.

'You don't say,' Erina replied. 'We all need sleep. We'll pick it up again tomorrow, shall we? Think the best thing we can do right now is to let him settle down. Poor thing's jumpier than a hyrax in a fungit den.'

The next morning, the first thing they did was check on their new guest. Though, technically, Sam had already done so when he woke up, which was way too early by Erina's standards. By now, the suns had, at least, cleared the mountain tops.

'Any better?' she asked as she put a boot up on the first rung of the fence around the paddock and leaned forward and partly over it. It creaked a bit.

The fence wasn't very high. It certainly wasn't higher than even the average horse could jump without effort. One intent on escaping would have cleared it in an instant. It was there more as a definition of space, separating it into the "inside" and "outside" of the paddock in a way that inside and outside the yard should have been but wasn't because most of it was grass just like everything else around here, though, by now, mostly consisting of worn paths crisscrossing it.

If the fence had been any lower, Sam wondered if he'd have stumbled over it when out walking. Probably not. It wasn't that small. But he'd certainly caught Erina walking "into" it — though she did that with a lot of things. Trees. Tables. People.

At least the latter got out of the way if they had any sense.

It *was* relatively new in comparison to some of the other structures around the stable, having been completed only after Sam's arrival.

It would have been easier to build out of premanufactured semblance wood planks, but as that would have meant having to lug everything all the way from the outside of the Valley, Erina had made do with what had been locally available. As such, the whole thing, posts included, were more of an interwoven collection of very young saplings stripped of their branches.

As planks they left a lot to be desired.

To someone from a larger facility it would have looked more like a holding area for something a lot smaller than a horse. Erina wasn't sure why she'd bothered starting it. It wasn't as if Harlan needed it. The trias wandered around as he pleased, and as it turned out, Wave Rock didn't stray far from Sam at any given time.

But, here it was. And, more than that, it now contained a horse. Sort of.

The black, horned, horse was huddled in a corner. The one furthest away from the two of them. He didn't seem to have gained as much energy back after a night's rest as either of them had expected.

At the moment he was doing his best to ignore them. Maybe if he didn't move they wouldn't be able to see him?

'Not the friendliest type, eh?' Erina mumbled. 'Can hardly blame you, can I? The last twenty-four hours must have been … intense … in all sorts of ways — none of them good.'

'At least he's not an overgrown puppy,' Sam said.

'Seranthiem, really? I expected better from you.'

'My apologies, My Lady.'

Sam made a small bow while simultaneously side-eying Harlan, who was watching intently. Ears pricked forward and neck arched, he'd been made to wear a halter and stand in his box. He didn't much like being tethered to anything, but was putting up with it … for now.

He didn't think he'd been overly excited and intimidating the newcomer through sheer joy at being able to make a new friend. As it was, he pulled the lead rope tight, trying to get as close as possible.

Harlan wasn't used to being tied up or shut away. It rarely ever happened and it was, usually, always for a good reason*. Like that time they'd been overrun by growling, snarling, voices, in the dark.

It meant that somewhere something fun … or exciting … *or dangerous* was happening and he wasn't there. The trias stomped his hooves and whinnied.

Harlan's continued "behaviour" was making the newcomer nervous. Well, more nervous than he already was. His eyes darted around, making sure the other one, Wave Rock, hadn't moved.

He hadn't. The dun was placidly munching on some hay sprinkled with

* Except the vet.

cut carrots and was entirely content with ignoring the commotion in the absolute certainty that it was nothing to do with him.

If it meant more horses around, then that was fine with him. If it didn't, he was fine with that, too.

The one not fine with it was the black shadow trying to make himself even smaller than usual. Sam didn't blame him. Harlan was a sweetheart once you got to know him, but he was a lot of horse in a small package, doubly so when he got excited (which was often).

'Well, we've given him some food and water,' Erina said. 'Guess we'll just have to see if he decides which he likes and if he wants to stick around. Not much else we can do right now.'

Sam nodded. 'He has some cuts I'd have liked to treat, but until he's comfortable with us, I fear that would only make things worse, not better.'

'Not like we can just call the vet out here. Bit of a commute, that.'

'No sedatives in medicine cabinet?'

'For a *horse*? No.'

'No reason to stress him out further then,' Sam said. 'Let us keep an eye on him and come back in a couple of hours.'

There was really nothing else for it. Until their four-legged visitor was more comfortable with either one or both of them there really wasn't much they could do but to take things one small step at a time. Though, maybe it was a good idea to take Harlan out and let him run off some of that excess energy … and then keep him on the other side of the stable for a while.

As such, for the next few days they made only limited amount of progress. The black stallion gradually came to not be as bothered with them, but while he started eating, it didn't seem to do as much for him as it should.

'Either he's more drained than I thought or something's wrong,' Erina pointed out.

'Worms?' Sam asked.

'Hope not,' Erina grimaced. 'We should have some tests in the medicine cupboard. Let's go get one. There's got to be something wrong … this isn't just anxiety. He doesn't mind us anymore. He even let me pet him for a moment yesterday.'

For a while it felt as if time was simultaneously flying by *and* standing still. The heaviness of deep summer was already upon them. Which was nice and all, it wasn't as if the heat was oppressive or anything. Sure, some days it could be a bit sweltering if you didn't like turning into a soggy sock, but mostly it was just warm enough that it was pleasant to do even heavier work — as long as you didn't do it right in the middle of the day or stayed in the shade.

Of the horses, Wave Rock didn't seem bothered either way, which made a lot of sense to Sam seeing as to where the horse had grown up. Their newest arrival, however, did not seem to enjoy the warm weather one bit.

While the be-horned black stallion had perked up a bit from when he'd first arrived and the gates to the paddock had been thrown open, he wasn't what you'd call energetic. Especially not during the day. He didn't merely seek out shade whenever he could but positively hid in the coolest, dampest, areas around the stable he could find.

Quite often, if they had to go look for him, they'd find him standing in the thickest shade the willow trees could cast over one of the nearby streams, hooves and hocks immersed in the cold water. Sometimes he'd even try to roll around in it, which they really weren't large enough for.

He livened up considerably during the evenings as the cooler, more moist, air drifted down from the mountains and out of the forests where it had been hiding from the suns.

In that, the black stallion reminded Seranthiem a bit of his current employer, who most definitely perked up around the time the pesky bits of gas (her words) gave up on the day and went to bed.

As it was currently almost mid-day, the midges were buzzing around like anything, and everything was getting brighter and brighter, the five horned horse was nowhere in sight if standing the stable yard.

It wasn't, however, him that Sam was out here looking for. His ears picked up on the possible location of Erina long before his eyes did. Unless a monkey* had gotten into one of the toolboxes, grabbed a wrench, and was hammering away like anything.

The irregular sounds led the way for Sam, who ended up coming around

* Did they Valley have even have those?

the corner in time to catch Erina picking a six inch nail from her mouth, placing it against one of the wooden beams balancing against each other over the front door to the main house, and then hitting it very hard with a hammer as if it had personally offended her.

Now, he'd have had no trouble doing that himself, if asked. He would even have brought a ladder if she'd insisted on doing it herself *and told him in advance.*

Erina hadn't bothered with a ladder. Nor had she shimmied up the side. Nope. She was standing, as if it was another Tuesday, on Harlan's back.

The trias stallion was standing surprisingly patiently up against the wall, right below the roof over the entrance. Judging from, well, everything, Sam surmised that this wasn't the first time he'd been asked to provide some additional height.

Harlan would do almost anything if there was a treat in there for him, except stand still … usually.

'What? It was faster,' Erina replied when a rather displeased Sam told her just what he thought of what she was doing.

For once, the hint of disapproval graced his otherwise pale, serene, features.

'What?' Erina said, louder this time. 'It was coming loose.'

'It really should—

'What was I supposed to do? Wait until it fell on my head? Don't you think we've had quite enough of things collapsing on us around here?'

'It would be better if—

That's all Sam managed before the world suddenly turned upside down. Not *his* world, but certainly *a* world. One moment Erina was standing casually on a nice, safe, horseback, one hand on the beam. The next she was very definitely on the ground.

Most of what could be said lay in between those states was a very loud, "Ouff!"

'That didn't hurt at all,' Erina gasped. Her chest felt as if it was trying to implode.

When everything finally stopped spinning and her eyeballs were no longer attempting to escape from her head, taking a moment to reorient herself, Erina narrowed her eyes, staring at the beams she'd been working on, as if daring them to follow her example.

They stayed up.

'Well, that's good of them I suppose. Having those landing on me would have been quite unpleasant.'

'Everything alright, My Lady?' Sam asked, worriedly, having hurried forwards. He held out a hand, offering her a hand up, which she accepted.

'No permanent harm done,' Erina replied, brushing herself off. 'That was not *fun*. And this is going to leave a mark,' she grimaced, poking at where her shirt had torn. 'Anyway, pass me the miniature pickaxe, will you?'

'The what?'

'That ... square looking hammer over there.'

'You mean the tack hammer, My Lady?'

Erina sighed and went to pick it up herself. 'I know what it does, Sam. I know what it looks like. I know how to use it. I don't need to remember its name.'

Seranthiem, after quite a bit of convincing, managed to divest his employer of said hammer, which she had still been gripping tightly, *and* to take a break in the kitchen while *he* fixed the porch roof over the main entry.

'*Before* you succeed in giving me a heart-attack!' as he put it once Erina was out of ear-shot. 'Honestly, would it kill you to ask for help once in a while?'

The first thing he did was to go and fetch an actual ladder. The second was realizing that it was a lot easier to work on the whole thing from above, so he climbed onto the roof instead.

A good thing there was barely any slant to it, just a gentle incline. It still came to a point but there wasn't much space for an attic.

Did they even have an attic for that matter? He'd never seen a hatch or anything. It could be something you couldn't ordinarily access. At the moment, did it matter?

As it turned out, the porch debacle wasn't the only thing he discovered. After repairing the porch roof he brought the find back with him, tucking it under one arm while climbing back down.

'Sam, it's striking,' Erina gasped, as he showed it to her.

‘It is very beautiful,’ Sam agreed. ‘Still, I would like to know why it was there.’

Erina carefully reached for the feather Seranthiem was holding. He relinquished it without a word.

She stroked it with a finger. It felt soft to the touch. Soft and a little puffy towards the point of the quill. Mostly a generic brown but a lighter, pale cream at the puffs, and with the tip being all black, it would have made an excellent fan.

‘This didn’t come from any bird I know,’ Erina said. ‘Where did you find this?’

‘Up near the knock,’ Sam replied. It was stuck near the chimney.’

‘Okay. Next question. *What* is it?’

‘As the long term resident, I was hoping you would be able to tell me, My Lady.’

‘It’s a feather,’ Erina said, flatly. She tapped the point against her chin. ‘That’s not what I meant.’

‘On that we’re in agreement, yes,’ Sam nodded. ‘Anything else?’

‘It’s absolutely freaking ginormous!’

‘So, the Valley does not have birds of prey of roc like proportions that you, through no fault of your own, have failed to disclose up until now?’ Seranthiem asked, a clear note of disapproval ringing in his voice.

The idea that something with wing feathers this large could have been watching him while out riding … at the house … in the fields. He repressed a shudder. It made him extremely uncomfortable.

If something like that attacked him, things could get … ugly. Sam restrained a wince from flying across his face. A couple of his pale fingers twitched.

‘*I’ve* certainly never seen any,’ Erina replied, affronted. ‘Something this large must be visible from quite the distance.’

‘I suppose it could be a ground dweller,’ Sam said. ‘Doubtful, but possible.’

Judging from his tone he didn’t believe that any more than she did, Erina thought. The reason why was obvious.

‘Highly unlikely,’ Erina agreed. ‘Not unless they love jumping around on roofs. Suppose it's possible the wind blew it in, but I doubt it. I think something's been spying on us.'

'That is becoming … somewhat of a trend,' Sam said and sighed, clearly not enjoying that thought at all.

❋❋❋

When Sam woke up the next morning and checked on all the horses (which was usually the first thing he did outside the house), their new "friend" was nowhere in sight. Any of the morning's chores failed to locate the black stallion anywhere in the immediate area around the stable.

By the time Erina moseyed out of her own bed it was in time to catch sight of all of them at the edge of the field beyond, peeking out from within the woodland.

The first few days after that the feed-buckets they'd been putting out had been sort of knocked over, as if someone was investigating them, hoping to find something else hidden within amongst all the oat and barely.

Now they were coming up empty. Someone was eating it, but it didn't look like it was the black shadow. At least, not all of it.

'Harlan,' Erina sighed.

'It could merely be a deer, or several, My Lady,' Seranthiem suggested, walking over once he spotted her.

Erina had her doubts. 'It's possible,' she acknowledged, reluctantly. 'So what *does* he like to eat?' she asked of the world. 'Thornbushes?'

'Does explain why he's so skinny,' Sam mused, picking up the bucket and examining it. 'The worm-tests all came back negative. We've tried different combos, but it doesn't seem he's overly interested. A picky eater, perhaps?'

'We're missing something, I'm sure of it,' Erina insisted.

'Clearly,' Sam agreed. 'Question is what?'

The water was hardly tastier than that in the nearby brook, though Harlan certainly had a fascination with it when presented with it in a bucket that'd made you think otherwise. So that part was understandable. And the new one, he did drink from the buckets they put out … on occasion.

The mix of feed was turning out to not be enticing enough to be preferred over the lush mix of grasses and other plants growing everywhere here, free for the munching.

Assuming he ate those.

Erina couldn't vouch for that it tasted better. One of many things she didn't include on her menu was grass or all that many vegetables at all, actually. But it was more nutritious (oat cookies were yummy) and, from what she could tell, the new arrival certainly needed to extra energy and bulk. While not skeletal it wasn't hard to see which way the wind was blowing.

He'd clearly bulked out a bit since first arriving at High Fyelds. But, even with that, there seemed to be something lacking.

As the days passed on by, it turned out the reason was obvious … once they'd all gotten more comfortable around each other and the horned shadow actually began letting them close. Not just for the occasional pet, either. Once he'd discovered the joy of brushing, there was no going back.

'So, fangs *and* molars?' Erina said, tossing the body brush she'd been using in a bucket full of different brushes. 'That explains a lot.'

Sam, meanwhile, was leaning with his back against the inside of the paddock fence. He offered their new friend a treat, which was gracefully accepted … snatched out of the air, actually.

'But no claws,' he said, glancing down at the black horse's hooves. They were the right shape for a horse. Nothing strange there. 'Quite the enigma, aren't you?' he said, softly.

The horse flicked a long, pointed, ear in his direction, considered if they were likely to toss them something else and, when not, contently returned to tearing small chunks off the undersized, skinned, Kopkapi.

Normally, the small deer-like critter was about the size of a dog*. This one, even before half of it had disappeared down the long, muscular, gullet, might have passed for a terrier at best.

'Oversized hamster's more like it,' Erina snorted amusedly when Sam pointed that out.

'No wonder you were so skinny when we found you,' Seranthiem mumbled. 'You require a diet that includes meat, but you're not actually able to "catch it" on your own, are you?'

* Though seeing some of the dogs she'd had, Erina didn't think that was the best comparison.

'At least not regularly enough,' Erina agreed. 'No wonder, with all that extra hair. He looks so much better now, don't you think?'

She let her eyes run over the black horse's body, adjusting views and opinions on his shape to go along with this new information. Mane and tail were still long, but they were the elegant type of long now, not the "entangle your limbs if you move" type.

'Mind you, I would have preferred if we found out by you *not* eating *our* dinner!' she said, arms crossed.

Once they learnt what their new friend actually needed to eat to have a *proper* diet rather than merely one he could barely survive on, the horse began filling out properly.

Bony edges became rounded. Slack skin grew taught once more. The coat lost its dull tones. Sleek lines began to appear as, with a source of food, he began moving about at more than a sad, exhausted, shuffle.

Soon enough, the new one had become the lithe, black, shadow they'd first taken him for. But, rather than slinking about in the night like a prowling ghost he seemed to prefer hiding in the bushes and watching … everything. It was as if his curiosity was in a constant battle with his caution.

Soon his favourite way of "acquiring" food on his own was by grazing with the others, then pouncing on some unsuspecting little critter hopping around in the tall grass.

'Well, he's fast,' Erina said one day, watching the black horse disappear around a corner in hot pursuit of a bunny.

'And very jittery,' Sam observed, picking up the bucket of liquidized manure. Erina's had sloshed all over her boots, much to her disgust, but his remained as full as when he'd first filled it. Possibly this was helped by that he hadn't actually filled it to the brim in the first place.

'Unlike Harlan, I don't think I'll ever need to shoo him away from trying to follow us into the house,' Erina said, trying not to breathe in the smell.

'You mean, follow *you* into the house,' Sam corrected. As friendly as the trias was, he was very much a one person horse. 'Next time we have a roast, I will enjoy seeing you being quite wrong about that,' Seranthiem chuckled.

'Either way, it's nice seeing them all getting along.'

'True.'

When neither of them were there, the black stallion would attach himself to Harlan or Rocky. Harlan was friendly to anyone — once he'd gotten used to having said someone around and deemed them safe that was — and Wave Rock was so stoic that, at this point, Erina wondered if he'd been an actual rock in a previous life. From what she'd seen so far she wondered if he'd do more than snort disdainfully if they were attacked by a bear or simply wait for his person to do something about it.

The second, most likely, she guessed. She'd gotten the impression that he'd follow Seranthiem through fire and water should the man ask it of him.

But it was, when it all came down to it, just a guess. There hadn't been any incidents, so far, that actually proved it. Not to *that* degree. She hoped they wouldn't have any. Nice and quiet with moderate excitement, that was enough for her right now.

Not that they needed to worry about things like bears. As far as she could tell, the Valley didn't have any. There'd been one or two encounters with creatures that she'd first mistaken for bears, true. One of them had turned out to be a huge red kelpie. The, essentially, giant otter had chased them for quite a bit as she recalled.

And the second? Well, that had been more of a kitchen autopsy, really. There was also the small fact that it had been quite fried even before she'd started carving it up. Nothing like living through a lightning storm on List-maker to teach you to keep your head down* when the weather got electric. But the ones in the Valley could be lethal, too, if you were unlucky.

Some of them got really charged up … sometimes almost out of nowhere.

'Still not sure what *that* was, but it *was* tasty,' Erina mumbled to herself.

* And preferably all other bits, too if you had any sense. Indoors. Deep in a mountain. And it *still* echoed and the air still tasted like metal. Which was impressive, seeing as the surface of D'hana Pin's fifth moon was, literally, mostly consisting of an ocean of liquid methane. i.e. quite lacking in either mountains or indoors…

HOLLOW'S FALL

'Get out of my face,' Erina said, trying to sidestep the shadow's neck and chest while he was nosing at the saddle she'd just put on Harlan. 'I still need to strap up the girth you silly goose and I'd rather not end up a human kebab, thanks.'

Praise be that Harlan was taking it all in stride. Not only was he waiting, patiently, for her to finish tacking him up (which made a nice change to how often he considered it an opportunity to play tag) but he didn't let the curiosity of their new friend annoy him.

'It is as if he knows that acting up around him could end up getting his favourite person speared, My Lady,' Sam said, showing one of his rare smiles.

Erina smacked her face into the saddle and groaned, 'Not you, too!'

Sam chuckled lightly.

'Anyway, we can't keep calling him "the new one",' Erina said as they finished preparing the two other horses for their next outing.

Sam completely agreed. Settling on a name, however, was a lot more difficult than deciding that they needed one. Which kind of surprised them both as it wasn't something either of them tended to have a problem with when it came to anything else.

Of course "thingy" didn't count. It could be used for … well … everything. As long as whomever you were talking to (yourself included) knew what you meant, you were golden.

But, while they'd both known the black, horned, horse for a while now, neither could think of an overwhelming characteristic, trait, or association that *worked* as a name once you said it out loud.

Or, when you then looked over to where the "horse" in question was snoozing in the shade, just didn't fit. "Shadow" had a nice ring to it, but even Erina felt it was a bit on the nose. It was a great name, it just wasn't him.

'We did find him in a hole in the ground,' Erina mused.

'A large subterranean network of interconnected caves, caverns, and tunnels is hardly how I would refer to as a "hole",' Sam said, his lips turning into a thin line.

'Potatoe, potato.' Erina shrugged. 'Same thing in the end.'

'You want to name him "*Hole*?"' Sam asked, hoping he was hearing things wrong.

'Of course not,' Erina scoffed. 'That was an observation, not a suggestion. Let me think some more, alright?'

'What do you think of Hollow?' Erina asked.

As far as Sam was concerned, it was simply a different spin on the same word — at least in this case.

The black horse also seemed unimpressed. There was not even a tail flick in response. Though that might have to do with that, seeing how long they were taking finishing up the preparations to move out, he'd actually gone to sleep next to the stable wall. The faint breeze occasionally sent ripples through his mane, making the red ends dance.

'Not where I was going,' Erina said. 'Still doesn't feel *quite* right, though.'

Even Sam agreed with that, though he didn't say anything. They watched the black horse sleeping, looking relaxed and safe, while gathering their thoughts and ideas.

Erina pulled down the stirrups of Harlan's saddle, checking the buckles as she went. The last thing she needed was them breaking on her due to wear and tear.

'Hollow's Fall.'

Sam glanced up and over, from where he'd been about to swing into the saddle himself. 'Hmm? What was that?' he asked.

'Hollow's Fall. That's … perfect,' Erina said, letting the words roll over her tongue as if tasting them. 'It's very … fitting*.'

'Sounds depressing,' Sam said. He didn't want to say it, but it brought back memories. Bad memories. 'But, he seems to like it. 'I suppose that's the important part.'

'Maybe it'd be more honest to say he isn't protesting,' Erina said, eyeing up the sleeping horse. 'On account of not hearing it, I mean.'

'There are times when honesty is not the best course of action,' Sam countered.

Not that either of them would actually use his full name most of the time. By the end of the week Sam was already grateful that Erina hadn't shortened it down to Hol, or Holly. A tendency she had with a lot of names, his included.

Hollow didn't seem to mind either way. Soon enough he was responding to it as if he'd been named that his whole life.

❊❊❊

'Whoah! Take it easy there,' Erina called out as Hollow rounded the corner to the back of the stable at a trot.

The black horse slammed on the breaks.

'Almost pierced me there,' Erina muttered, rubbing her arm.

She was still getting used to having to dodge the five pronged equine pitchfork. Sometimes not by much. Sometimes not at all.

Both Harlan and Wave Rock were currently enjoying their food just a little further away — though the portion sizes during summer was more like dessert rather than a three course meal, seeing how everywhere around them the ground positively burst with vibrant, and energy rich, vegetation.

The biggest danger there was Harlan forgetting he was made of lean muscles and mobbing her when getting overexcited that he'd get an extra treat. She'd learnt to safeguard her own feet. They did not enjoy getting stepped on.

Feeding time wasn't necessarily the *only* time the now lithe, black, shadow got fed. Or, more accurately, got around to feeding himself. Hollow still couldn't hunt properly to save his life, but was getting in plenty of practice chasing the smaller local wildlife about. As far as a source of juicy meats,

* Though she didn't explain *why* it was fitting, in hindsight, it made perfect sense to Sam.

he'd found much easier prey.

Best of all, he didn't need to do any running to catch it. Until now that was. And he wasn't running after it. He was running *away* from it … after a successful heist.

'Aha!' Erina exclaimed, catching sight of what was dandling from the horse's mouth. 'So *that's* where my steaks've been disappearing off to!'

Hollow looked guilty. Guilty of being caught, that was. Blood was dripping from his curled lips. The last piece of cured ham was slurped up, disappearing with a "schlup" sound through the elongated jaw.

'I suppose it's not enough that Harlan stakes out where we hide the treats? Now you're stealing our cold-cuts? Bad Horse! That was supposed to be dinner! *My* dinner!'

Erina was standing straight, hands on her hips, and a frown going all the way from her forehead to her lips.

The words might have been intimidating, if you weren't able to read the rest of the languages spoken.

Hollow's ears flickered, then he nickered, happily, walked over and tried to nuzzle her.

'Got a taste for the good life already, boy? Woah! Careful,' Erina yelped. 'You know, it's great that you're getting friendlier, but can we do this without the threat of impalement?'

Considering that the horns were sitting on *his* head, Hollow seemed to forget about them frequently. As a result, he often got lodged in things or knocked things over. On one memorable occasion, he got stuck in a door, head first*.

'This does explain why the idea of a bit never appealed,' Sam said as he watched from the side. He'd gotten a good look at Hollow's mouth as the horse yawned. It was definitely not built like an ordinary horse's.

'Few predators do, Erina acknowledged. 'Like them, I mean. No matter, it's not like that's a new one. Just a bit of a surprise that that's why the food's been going missing. I'm kind of relieved, to be honest. I was afraid it might be rats.'

She turned back to Hollow, who was looking curiously between the two

* The door *had* probably deserved it, Sam thought. Erina certainly swore at it enough.

of them, not entirely sure if he was in trouble or not.

'We'll have to be more careful about locking up the doors,' Erina said. 'Hopefully you can't shrink and fit through the windows. Bit of a chameleon, aren't you?'

Erina's voice dropped to something more familiar and teasing and Hollow began to relax. An ear flicked forwards. He tap-danced, hoping that, since they weren't mad that he'd be able to mob them for some extra tasties. Harlan had the right idea there, he thought.

'A somewhat unusual circumstance, My Lady,' Seranthiem acknowledged. 'There have been numerous nightmares for whom the same could be said. There is, usually, a solution. Perhaps we can look for some that someone else has already found, next time we leave Darklight Valley.'

'True,' Erina admitted. 'But it's not like we need them. Bits, I mean. Convenient for directions, true … but even a needleship can be flown with a frozen joystick … if you know how.'

She was right, Sam knew that. He didn't, technically, need one, either*. While he did use a perfectly ordinary snaffle with Wave Rock, it was because ir allowed for more subtle communication when that was needed. There were definitely times when using your voice was a bad idea.

And vice versa, for that matter. But that wasn't the issue at hand, he reminded himself.

For just moving about the general stable area or anywhere he felt it was safe, a plain halter was more than enough. There were times he didn't even bother with that. Or a saddle.

Erina, meanwhile, wasn't a bareback sort of person at all. While using a halter instead of a bridle was fine, just having something in her hands kept her happy. The lack of any saddle, to put things in perspective, tended to make her very *unhappy*.

At first, Sam had thought that it was a balance issue, but after seeing her casually traipsing along on foot thick wooden beams with nary a care in the world as they were building the roof of one of the new outbuildings meant to become a new tack room, that idea didn't appear to hold much weight any more.

* For his *horse*…

Though it was always with his heart in his throat that he watched that sort of thing happen. It was fine when he did it. He trusted himself. When it came to things like that, he definitely didn't trust Erina. After all, he frequently witnessed her walking *into* things.

Not very often had he caught her, surprisingly enough, walking *off* them...

'A diverse diet for our little omnivorous sneak thief, then,' Erina said, giving Hollow a number of long, slow, pets on his slender neck.

'If he's staying permanently, perhaps we should prepare a box for him. And train him,' Sam suggested, though judging from his tone it was less of a suggestion and more a desperate hope that Erina would come to realize this herself.

He needn't have worried.

'You did say you thought the place was lacking a cat or dog,' Erina said. She pointed at Hollow and grinned mischievously, her fingers doing the silent equivalent of "taa daa!"

'That is not what I meant, as you are well aware.'

'Ah, Sam ... lighten up a little. This isn't the bridge of a planetary cruiser or a day at the races. You don't need to be so formal all the time.'

Sam mulled over this for a while, silence stretching out between them. 'This seems ... very unlikely,' he said, eventually.

***

Aside from brief interludes from the agents of chaos, life mostly went on as usual at High Fyelds once Hollow's Fall had settled in.

With two pairs of hands, the work was a lot easier, Erina thought. She'd gotten so used to doing everything herself, or simply not being able to do them at all, that it was hard to adjust how she thought and planned. She'd never been much of a team player and when she'd been required to be on one, it was only ever for short term assignments.

This shift to not only constantly having someone else around was hard enough. Trying to get her mind to plan for things "as four hands" was a struggle.

Turned out there was also a lot more to do*. It was like when receiving a knitted jumper from your favourite aunt and, when accidently pulling on what you thought was a loose threat, finding that a moment later you were up to your ears in yarn … but there was no longer any sign of the jumper.

There was *never* enough time.

'Come on. Might as well get this show on the road,' Erina said. Taking a few light hops, she swung up into the saddle, shifting around a bit to get comfortable. Collecting the reins she nudged Harlan into a trot. Not that the four-legged bundle of energy needed it, he was moving the moment he felt the weight on his back.

As usual, Sam's entry into the saddle could be described as more of an elegant glide upwards. Wave Rock, however, stood stock still until his rider clicked him into motion with his tongue.

At which point the dun picked up speed to catch up with his friend.

Sam had gotten used to these excursions.

Sometimes they were to acquire things for the stable — those tended to be shorter. Only once in a while did you have to stay out overnight.

Sometimes they were to check up on … things. It wasn't always clear to him what was being checked-up on, but he expected it would make sense with time.

Like that time they'd climbed all the way to the top of Mount Skutla only for Erina to take a look around and inform him that yes, everything seemed fine, and headed on back down again.

That had not been a short trip. The mountain was very barren towards the top, mostly rock and stone, with the occasional windswept, often dead, tree. Erina had told him to watch out for the ice, but it hadn't been until reaching the peak that Sam had understood what she meant. Rather than coming to a point, Mount Skutla had been partially hollowed out. In its heart now sat a small, cirque glacier, surrounded by jagged teeth where the mountain had crumbled. That had been a bit of a surprise for him, Sam had to admit.

He'd have called it an ice-volcano, except he'd already encountered real ones elsewhere.

* Sam had a very different idea about what constituted an inconvenience than Erina.

He'd always enjoyed them. The outings, that was, not the volcanoes. Riding through lands devoid of people and simply relaxing to the nature living around him had always been one of his favourite things.

There were no mountains on today's itinerary. Not to ride up and into, at least. "Going around" was pretty much the only way you could move from one part of the Valley to another.

Sam wondered when he'd started drifting off, because they arrived at their goal a lot faster than he'd expected.

Glancing upwards, the great big skylights suggested it hadn't even been a couple of hours, yet it should have taken them half a day at least. By this point he'd been here long enough that this little shift merely had him shrug, putting it all down to "one of those things".

They had to have a name, Sam thought. The hilly plains that was the home to the largest herd of wild horses in Darklight Valley. It didn't.

Not yet, Sam told himself. One of these days he was going to sit down with the map he was working on and name the places he visited himself. At least that way *he* would know what he was talking about, even if no-one else did.

It didn't take long to spot the herd Erina had mentioned. The weather was nice, the day was young, and there were no predators about stalking anyone, and so they were having a spot of lunch, grazing on the freshest shoots they could find.

As a result, they'd spread out over a much wider area than normal. Not that it made a difference to the two riders.

The herd barely flicked even one lazy tail in their direction*. At this point they'd gotten so used to Erina and Harlan going about their business in the Valley that they more or less considered them fixtures in the landscape. Moving fixtures, true, but nothing to be bothered by.

Not that a rock that had been there for millennia wasn't quite capable of scaring the hooves off you at the wrong time. Or squash you. But it wasn't something you went around thinking about all the day.

The appearance of Seranthiem and Wave Rock had made them a little uneasy at first, but now, many months later, they'd gotten accustomed to them,

* In the direction of the petulant flies, that was another matter.

too.

Erina leant to the side, chatting with Sam, as they both rode "through" the herd of wild horses. Though "through" was a deceptive word. It wasn't as if anyone needed to get out of anyone else's way.

A second later and it was as if somewhere someone had flicked a switch. Heads snapped up. Neighing happened. And, with an impressive from stand-still to full throttle, the wild horses took off, galloping away, ears flat.

The sudden noise all around startled the two mounts, but once the herd had zoomed past them, they settled back down again. Albeit they were both a bit more restless now.

'What has *them* so spooked?' Sam asked, turning his entire shoulders to see better. Not catching sight of anything, he stood up in the stirrups for a better view.

As did Erina.

Both he and Wave Rock were taller than either Erina or Harlan on their own, though, to say nothing about together, and so had a distinct advantage in terms of their field of view.

This time it didn't help them. Sam didn't see anything that could have scared the wild horses that wouldn't also have bothered the ones they were riding.

Wave might not have reacted, but there was no force in the universe that would have kept Harlan from startling unless he'd received that memo beforehand, in writing, with the proper stamps and seals.

'There!' Erina called out.

Pointing almost behind them, Sam managed to catch a glimpse of something visible only for a second before it disappeared once more into one of the many depressions.

Erina put her head in her hands, knocking into an eye with the leather reins in the process.

'Oh bother,' she said, rubbing at it. 'That actually hurt. Sam, look who followed us.'

'Who?' Sam asked, before, a moment later, catching sight of their stalker as they, no longer trying to hide, was coming towards them, high stepping and tail streaming in the wind.

'Hollow? I should have noticed earlier.'

Erina chuckled, clearly amused. 'I assumed you *had* and just wasn't saying anything,' she admitted.

'But why would they be so bothered by Hollow as to run away,' Sam wondered as the black and red stallion trotted up to them, neck arched, and eyes glittering excitedly.

'Well, he *is* a predator,' Erina pointed out, as the horned horse nuzzled her boot. '*Technically*,' she added after one of those telling "looks" from her companion. She tried to shoo him off … with little effect.

Hollow seemed very happy now that he didn't need to sneak around. Instead, the black stallion gambolled around them like an excited foal … and with about as much control over his legs. He often seemed to forget how many he had when he was having fun.

'We're not far from where we're going,' Erina said, taking a deep breath. 'Come on. We might be able to finish up and start the return journey before dark, even with our current little ball of mischief getting us into trouble every step of the way.'

'You can't be certain of that?'

'Can't I?'

Choosing to take a sudden interest in checking the packs were tied on securely, Sam busied himself until he felt sure Erina had gotten any laughs out of her system.

'What are we doing, My Lady? You didn't say,' he asked.

If she had said, he'd forgotten. Which was, very much so, more embarrassing. Seranthiem suspiciously eyed the folded up hand shovels and jute sacks tied to the rest of their gear that they'd brought along.

Erina shrugged. 'You did say a while back that you wished the garden was bigger. Since we can't exactly just go order plants for delivery, I thought we'd go pick some things up the old-fashioned way.'

'Plants?'

Erina merely grinned at him.

'I'm trusting you'll know what to do with them once we actually have them. I've never been all that good with growing things*,' she said.

* Indeed, there were herbicides that worked slower than Erina when it came to killing plants.

Judging by his expression, Sam seemed excited by the thought. Next season there would be more ingredients. Fresh ones. Seranthiem smiled. That would make cooking a lot more fun.

And, if they had them at the stable, it'd bring some variety to the greenery, too.

He couldn't wait to see what they might dig up.

A few days later they returned back to the stable, having ended up being able to bring back even more than expected thanks to convincing Hollow to carry some make-shift packs made out of old jute. This included two small cherry trees, complete with soil, bobbing along on either side of his flank.

They had a few broken branches from when they'd ended up meeting the earth the wrong way up when Hollow had gotten spooked once … or twice.

The rest of the haul was in better condition — and a lot smaller. Sam couldn't wait to start transplanting them into the garden. Their current "home" wasn't going to be enough for long.

There were a couple of things he needed to do first, and so, at the moment, Sam was leaning against one of the wooden work-horses around the back of the stables. One of several, it had a number of unfinished projects stacked against a nearby wall.

There was never enough time it seemed. For a place that was very "iffy" about the concept of time in the first place, it sure liked running out of it. This included right now, which was why he was ignoring all those other things that needed to be done.

'That does it, that's all the pause I can afford right now,' Sam mumbled. 'Back you go.' Squaring up his shoulders, he picked up what he'd come here for and returned to where he'd come from.

The garden.

It wasn't far. Nothing around the stable was. High Fyelds wasn't exactly large.

The vegetable garden around the "back" (if such a concept existed given High Fyelds' layout) was separated from the stables by the new paddock, a fence, and, for good measure, a small hedge of edible berry bushes he had yet to learn the name of. The edge wasn't there for decoration. The bushes were part of the garden. It was merely a defining edge.

Which, right now, was the only one it had. The other ones clearly sort of blended into the landscape around it. Sam wasn't entirely sure if this was intentional … or not.

They were the only berries that had already been here before. Almost everything else in the plot was of the vegetable persuasion — although in some cases the Exgees would have argued about what actually constituted a vegetable*.

But there were a lot of things on Casticia that couldn't clearly be separated into the neat categories that the people had inherited from their Earthly origin. And that didn't even account for how their own plants had changed after generations on-board a spaceship.

They would have been infuriated with Erina, Sam imagined. As far as she was concerned, if it grew in the ground, it was a plant. Unless it was a mushroom. She seemed to have quite the vendetta against mushrooms, and refused to eat them, even sautéed with garlic.

The current garden wasn't very impressive, even though Sam had tried spending some time making improvements. For his own sake if no-one else's.

So far, Erina had stuck to things she'd found easy to grow†. A sort of minimum effort — maximum return situation.

True, they were all looking a little … sad, despite that the other important variable was; hardiness. If the plants required a delicate touch or precise conditions, they were out.

Much easier to go around the Valley and pick things where they grew, Erina thought. Sure, it took more time, but didn't she have plenty of that?

Quite a large patch was dedicated solely to potatoes despite that Erina really didn't like them. There were at least three different types that matured at different times of the year. They'd been eating the ones whose stems lay dried on top of the soil, being the only ones that had matured yet.

Erina had recognized that she needed a staple crop. The idea of having to supplement what she hunted with nutrilicious bars was horrid enough to have spurred even her into action.

* Generally it was considered that "walking away" was an instant disqualifier.

† i.e. that not even she had managed to kill.

Rice took way too much effort and a whole system designed behind them for optimum yields. Also, Erina tried keeping things in the ground for as long as possible as a sort of auxiliary root-cellar. That way they kept longer. The downside was that they also got a lot more, eh, chewy, towards the end.

Though, in the case of the cabbages all that meant was that the last ones went to feeding the local wildlife, because by the time she got around to eating those they were more like round balls of wood than anything fit for human consumption.

'Still better than having to eat a nutrilicious bar,' Sam said, while Erina made a disgusted face.

'Just the thought, urgh,' she said and shuddered.

In that they were in perfect agreement.

One set of green beans were still little more than green shoots poking through the soil in several rows. She'd been late getting those into the ground. Meanwhile, the salad and the honey melons were growing like crazy, their extension vines threatening to overwhelm the rest of the patch. One reason why they were eating so much of the dratted things at the moment.

She'd never thought she'd be sick of melon. Rich. Sunripe. Sweet as honey. Melon.

On the other side, several of the second planting of the carrots were sad, drooping, images of themselves. There, at least, Erina felt she wasn't at fault.

Glaring down at them, she still hadn't made up her mind about them. Harlan loved them, true. But growing them meant waging a constant, multipronged, war against the local hyrax warren, who'd taken a shine to the newly arrived food so readily available.

Maybe Hollow could help there? If he could learn to actually catch the wily little critters, that was.

Sam nodded, satisfied. There was still a lot of work to do, but it was progressing well.

'We'll pick some of the beans for dinner,' he said. 'After that, we better begin transplanting all those lovely new plants, shall we?'

'We can probably leave the trees for tomorrow,' Erina said, giving a nod towards where they'd leaned the two large jute sacks against a wall.

There was the tiniest of wooden sheds at the bottom of the "garden". Aside from the new trees, a hoe was leaned against another wall, still not cleaned from the last time it had been used.

The only wheelbarrow, rusted and worn, stood beside it. It was, currently, partly filled with the nest of a hedgehog that had moved in last winter. Despite, numerous times, telling the creature it wasn't welcome, it still hadn't left. Erina suspected it knew she wasn't serious when she told it to get lost.

'We'll have to add a new one to the list of items to pick up on the next outing,' she said. 'Unless you think you can build one?'

'Possibly best to leave that to the professionals,' Sam suggested. 'The rubber wheel is much easier to work over these grounds than a wooden one with spokes.'

'True, that. The ones on the wagons are plenty,' Erina agreed. Hands on her hips, she surveyed the patch.

'At least it looks better than last year,' she muttered to herself. 'And let's not even get started on the year before that.'

One reason, the biggest reason, for that was that Sam had been doing most of the looking after the garden, outside of picking things, ever since he first arrived. Even so, the current state of it had been paid in water, salt, and, when misjudging an evil looking briar, some iron as well.

The garden wasn't the only new arrival that needed tending to. Despite the seeming advantage of that the plants stayed in one place, Erina still preferred working with the other one.

Hollow nosed at the strange leather contraption currently draped over the top rung of the fence.

It smelled of sweat, leather, and horse. It should, he'd seen it in use. Of course he had. He still wasn't sure what it was supposed to be. It seemed to be needed to help the small two-legs glue themselves to Harlan's back? But then the tall one didn't always use one, so were they actually necessary? Or was that one of the differences between them? They smelled similar, but having been the only two-legs he'd ever encountered, Hollow figured that was how they were all supposed to smell like.

One smelled like the clouds before a storm. Lightning in a bottle. Contained. Electrifying. Dangerous. He liked it.

The other smelled of flax and cool mountain lakes. It was soothing but, for some reason, a little off-putting. Almost as if it was *too* calm.

On occasion, these leather-things would be attached, like leeches he supposed, to his new friends' backs. Unlike leeches, these things came off again without fuss. They didn't seem to hurt, which was another way they differed from the blood suckers.

If anything, whenever one of the two-legs brought one out (and didn't bring that foul-smelling stuff, too) Harlan and Wave Rock got very excited. Well, *really* excited in Harlan's case and a mild, yes-can-I-help-you-my-favourite-person type of excitements in terms of Wave.

He'd swear the dun stallion wouldn't react to a lava monster unless his person panicked first — which was *very* unlikely, from what he'd seen so far. The silver haired one seemed very responsible, Hollow thought. But if he was going to back anyone fighting a lava monster he'd pick whatever side the small one was on.

He must have let his imagination run away with him, because he was brought back to the here and now by a voice that managed to sound displeased even when speaking softly.

'Hollow! Stand still!' Erina admonished the black horse. 'It's not even a saddle. It's *just* a blanket.'

She held up the inoffensive, not quite square, piece of cloth. Had he imagined it as a big bad monster? Whoops.

Hollow sniffed at it cautiously, letting out a loud "harrumph".

It was a bit worn, frayed even, in places. The victim of numerous teeth. Harlan's scent was all over it. He'd seen the trias running around with it, often having snatched it from the fence or his person's hands.

It might have gone under that leather-thing, but not for a long time. It wasn't even the same pattern as the one Hollow saw him wear these days. But, he must have been wearing this one a lot in the past, for even now the scent on it was practically ingrained.

This made Hollow feel a little better. It wasn't something completely unknown.

That did *not* mean he was going to let anyone put it on *his* back. Weird bags was one thing, but this were something else entirely. For starters, it was someone else's. Where was *his*? Didn't he get one of his own? Wasn't he good enough to get his own?

What was this travesty?

There was another collection of loose straps of leather hanging from a fence post. If you didn't know, right now, you couldn't tell that it was a bridle.

The bridle itself was bitless. Though, compared to some things, even calling it a bridle was a bit of a stretch. Maybe they added pieces to it as you levelled up? Hollow wasn't sure how all of this was supposed to work.

This was something they'd done many times before and it never got more exciting. Hollow wondered when they'd actually get around to *doing* something.

❊❊❊

The late summer breeze lazed about, building personality. It touched a straw of grass here. Blew a ripple across a pond there. If it had been at the height of its powers, the standstill would have led to the day being absolutely sweltering.

Erina waved her hand in front of her face. As a fan it didn't really work. 'Talk about stuffy,' she complained. 'Maybe I should have woken up earlier.'

'It would have been cooler to do this, then,' Sam agreed.

No longer merely a background noise, the slow droning of insects, from the tiny gnats who were more seen than heard — if you were close enough — to the song of grasshoppers and everything in between, took over the day.

'Thankfully no oversized ones,' Erina said. 'Imagine bees the size of a horse?'

'Until just now, I hadn't,' Sam said.

There was the swish of a tail. Another one. Another tail. Another swish. Back and forth they went. The flies kept buzzing back. And if they were successfully swatted there was always another to take their place.

Harlan and Wave Rock were both munching on the supple grass in the upper field. Being a natural, wild, field, the many grasses reached their knees. As did many of the wildflowers and other things that grew in it.

Some of them were tasty. They both stayed away from the brightly coloured flowers that looked like if you'd tied several bells to a single stem because it made them all feel awful. Thankfully it wasn't poisonous to the touch, but they gave it a wide berth all the same.

Hollow's Fall couldn't care less. If anything, he enjoyed them. Which was probably why even the edges of the field had been stripped bare of the bright foxgloves.

'As if we needed more proof you're only equine-adjacent,' Sam had said when realizing why he hadn't needed to clear them out as per usual.

At the moment, Sam had retreated to the shade. The heat of the late summer suns was something you worked in only if you had to. Relaxing was something you did somewhere cooler and less prone to sting your eyes and give you a headache.

Normally, he wasn't bothered by it. Today, however, it was brighter, stronger, than usual.

Hence why he was currently leaning his back against the trunk of a young oak at the edge of one of the small untouched copses dotted around the far field. A book was splayed open over his knees, balancing precariously as his hands were otherwise occupied.

It was currently taking only part of his attention. The other was on where his hands actually were. With a feather touch, the tips of his fingers flew over the wooden flute, teasing music out of the air, while one eye was trained on the notes written down.

His silver hair was tied up in the customary high ponytail he favoured, though most of it was currently draped over one shoulder as it kept snagging on the bark.

The other eye, the one that wasn't reading, kept flitting back to the rest of the company. This was one of his favourite places around High Fyelds, and he didn't usually share it. But, then, he hadn't exactly invited them over.

'Why, you never told me you played,'* Erina said, sounding delighted at the discovery.

Why, he had no idea. It wasn't as if it was hard. Anyone could do it. Couldn't they?

* Yet another thing he'd left out of his resume.

‘I somehow always imagined you as more of a violin person,’ Erina admitted.

Sam tried not to shrug as to not shift the book out of position while taking one hand off the wooden flute. ‘I *can* play that,’ he said. ‘But I didn’t think bringing that along on a trek into the wild interiors of this place,’ he waved his hand over where they were, ‘was a particularly good idea.’

He refrained from adding that he wasn’t very good at it. Personally, he much preferring the soothing sounds of an erhu to the banshee shriek he’d managed to coax out of the one violin he owned.

In Erina’s imagination, he suspected *that* imagery would have been very different. The fiddler standing on a grey cliff’s edge. Maybe a waterfall in the background. The entire Valley stretched out before it. Playing for the sky and wind and clouds swirling dramatically in response.

That might not have been exactly what was going through her mind, but it was close enough. The image suited him, Erina decided and she told him so.

Sam was too polite to tell her what he thought about *that* idea.

One thing was certain, it was a sharp contrast to where they were now. A far more sedate, mundane almost, setting, sitting around and merely drinking the day in.

The notes he teased out of the flute were vibrant, almost alive, and somehow tinged with something that drove an ice-pick straight into your very soul.

FAST IS SLOW

Erina shortened the reins. Straightening up in the saddle, she felt the tension beneath her. Hollow had heard it, too.

Good. That meant she hadn't imagined it.

It wasn't the first time they'd been out together, thank goodness. She wasn't sure if she'd trust him to stay calm if something, well, *happened.* She liked him. Experiencing things from his back led you to see the Valley entirely differently than it did when she rode Harlan.

'Blast,' she muttered. 'Bad timing.'

Swivelling her head from side to side, she tried to make out where it had come from. What was it with mysterious sounds this season? Had they had a sale on them or something?

But, there was nothing. No betraying rustle in the foliage. No shifting in the bushes as if something was moving through them. No birds taking wing — well, more than normal.

The only thing that stirred was the slight breeze in the tree crowns far above. The light sprinkled down through them, but it didn't make any noise.

The mostly beech and ash trees out this way made this section of the woodlands lighter than many. They weren't deep in, either. Anything truly dangerous tended to remain … elsewhere. You were more likely to be run over — or through — by an angry herbivore than a predator around here. Yet, there were no signs of anything, other than Hollow pawing the ground, digging up patches of moss and grass and the occasional small bush.

Normally, she found this place light and airy. There was still plenty of sunlight coming in from between the leaves. Entire blue patches of sky. A perfect place for a spring ride, the new leaves still wet with the night's rain. Not bad for a picnic, either.

Today? Maybe going into the forest on a not-quite-trustworthy horse hadn't been a good idea? Lots of things spooked Hollow. Small things. Big things. Things that weren't even things. Right now all sorts of scenarios were running through Erina's mind about how he might react to something actually serious.

None of them ended well. Or, at least, not without effort on her part. Erina wasn't in general favour of effort. That was something that happened to other people.

'That's what I get for feeling overconfident, I suppose,' Erina muttered. She shifted the reins to one hand, the other now hovering over the hilt to her sword. 'And here our first solo had been going so well.'

Hollow snorted, nervously. His steps were getting stiffer and stiffer. Higher and higher. Even the leisurely walk was speeding up, becoming more of an I'm-getting-out-of-here but I'm not quite ready to run… just in case I'll run right *into* what I'm trying to escape.

His new muscles quivered.

'What is it, boy?' Erina asked, casually pretending she wasn't worried at all.

If she'd been alone she wouldn't have worried. The occasional bit of excitement was good fun. It wasn't as if the Valley was big on entertainment. You had to make your own.

When something jumped out at you trying to rip your throat out, Erina felt perfectly justified in returning the favour. Usually with a great deal more success*. She was far less concerned about what might be out there than she was about what might happen if Hollow freaked out.

A beastie she could handle. There she was allowed to fight back. With her luck she'd get knocked out by a low-hanging branch after her mount bolted.

* Minus the actual throat ripping. She had better things to do with her teeth.

Some of that "confidence" must have been contagious, for Hollow stopped trying to run away while not.

Maybe he remembered, in that moment, all those outings he'd shadowed his new friends and how, even when something *had* happened, there hadn't been anything to be afraid of?

Not that he was about to let *his* guard down. Running away was what had kept him alive so far*. He wasn't going to change years of instinct (or ingrained behaviour) over night.

Or several nights for that matter.

Erina leaned forward in the saddle, giving the black stallion several reassuring pats on the silken neck.

'Now, now, let's not get carried away here,' she said. 'I'm sure we'll find out who, or what, has been stalking us for the last ten minutes, I promise.'

Erina stared out into the forest, eyes turning into slits, and growled, 'And if that's you, Seranthiem, we're going to have *words*!'

The last bit was addressed to the forest in general or what might be lurking in it, whichever showed itself first. Whatever it was, it promised trouble.

It was, probably, a good thing for Sam that it wasn't him.

Where *was* Sam, anyway? She hadn't seen him all day. Had he mentioned going somewhere on his own? Erina couldn't recall.

'I do hope he hasn't gotten himself into trouble,' she muttered. 'I don't have time for this shit.'

Deciding to turn around and go a different way, she never did find out what had been lurking in the woods that day.

The far more concerning matter was that she didn't find Sam, either. Not on the way back. Not at the stables. By the time night fell, Erina had begun pacing.

By the time morning came around concern had turned to worry. After scouring the entire stable again (just in case) there was still no sign of him.

Erina's search circle expanded … and expanded … and expanded.

Still no sign of Sam.

It wasn't as if he was easy to miss. She wasn't going to mistake him for anyone else out here.

* Not that he'd been able to properly run for some time before joining High Fyelds.

'Where *is* he?' she asked Hollow. She'd dismounted to inspect a suspicious looking trail that, when viewed up close, turned out to be nothing of the sort.

'Not unless he part-times as an evil tree, lost control, and decided that having a small lunch snack on the go was the best idea ever'. Erina snorted. That didn't seem like Seranthiem even on his worst day.

Neither Harlan nor Hollow could do much to help there. She'd brought both horses this time around, a good thing as it turned out, as Harlan had ended up losing a small argument with the ground at one point. While he was, mostly, fine, or pretending to be, he couldn't disguise the limp. As such, Erina had been riding Hollow exclusively during the latter half of the day.

Riding him was fine. It was when you dismounted that you had to look out.

'Hey, careful with those!'

Erina yelped as she narrowly avoided getting speared as Hollow swung his head around to check what she was doing.

'Watch out you little maniac. Those things are sharp! I'm not a human shaped kebab, you know!' Erina scolded him lightly, trying to sound more serious than she was, while pushing the inquisitive muzzle away.

She'd long since gotten used to Harlan's insistence of trying to dig himself a spot under her arm. But that was a child's game compared to avoiding the pointed sabres that decorated Hollow's delicate head.

The black stallion turned two soulful, teal-blue eyes at her. Here, in the daylight, you had to squint to see that they were still glowing. Either that or they'd really dimmed down as of late.

Hollow was curious, much like Harlan — might be one reason why the two got along so well — but a whole lot more skittish. If something startled Harlan he might take off but, assuming something wasn't chasing him, he'd stop and wonder what the fuss had been more often than not before even leaving the stable yard.

Hollow, in comparison, just wouldn't stop running. He didn't go quite as far as he used to, but he certainly wasn't going to stick around to find out what had frightened him in the first place.

Right now they were both watching as Erina was examining the ground further. They, too, noticed that Wave Rock had come through here.

‘But where did he go?’ Erina asked the air. ‘It doesn’t seem he was going anywhere in a hurry, at the time these tracks were made anyway. He’s the only shoed horse in the entire Valley. There’s no mistaking those hoof-prints for anyone else’s.’

It took some time, weighing the different possibilities. There didn’t seem to be any urgency, unless it had happened after. What was the chance of that? It would explain why neither horse nor rider had returned home. But could she take that chance?

‘Sam, if I find out you’ve merely gone walk-about or something you’re in so much trouble,’ Erina growled. ‘Very well. Hollow. Harlan. Let’s head back home and get your leg looked at. Hollow, you and me are going to go on a little hunting trip tomorrow, okay?’

Hollow’s Fall wasn’t entirely certain what all this means, but he lipped Erina’s sleeve. His two-legs seemed awfully worked up about this whole thing.

‘Stop trying to eat my shirt, Hollow! Honestly, you’re picking up all the wrong habits from Harlan.’

Next morning, Erina had set the alarm to wake her up. Stopping by the kitchen, she put some more perishable foods in the satchel she’d prepared the night before, then headed straight out to the horses.

While both of them were happy to see her, Harlan was sulking a little. That was because he’d had to stay *home* last night. In his box.

He enjoyed it in the winter. It was nice and cosy. As Erina let him out this morning, he complained by ignoring her, going straight for the food. Two mouthfuls later and he was already butting his head against her back as she brushed down Hollow, tack ready on the side.

‘No Harlie, you need to stay home,’ Erina said and patted the trias affectionately on the neck, stroking his forehead, and twisting out some of the knots and tangles in the long black and white forelock that fell forwards when Harlan tried to push his muzzle into her face.

Harlan snorted. The idea of not being allowed to come along clearly annoyed him. For a moment he subtly eyed the paddock fence, seriously considering jumping over it. The gate didn't need to swing aside for him to get out. He'd done it before when he couldn't be bothered to walk around.

Then his leg twinged and he was reminded of why he wasn't the one wearing the saddle.

'Now, now. Don't be a silly. You just need a few day's rest and we'll be back by then,' Erina told him.

The tricoloured horse tossed his head impatiently. He didn't want to wait. He wanted attention *now*. This was boring. If he couldn't go anywhere, the least they could do was stay and keep him company.

'I'll be back, I promise. We won't be gone long. You'll have to leave this one to Hollow, okay?'

Erina gave Harlan a last pat from the other side of the fence, then swung into the saddle of the fully tacked up black stallion.

True, she'd needed to do a bit of walking first. He hadn't been standing exactly where Erina had left him — having wandered over to investigate a clearly superior lump of grass with some very intriguing stains on them.

'We're going to need to do some serious training with you,' Erina said, then clicked her tongue at him.

At least that cue Hollow picked up on. He fell into a trot and, after some further encouragement, a slow, loping, canter. The stables were soon far behind them.

The trail twisted and turned until there no longer was one. Soon Erina and Hollow had left the open space where High Fyelds was located*. Entering the nearby woodland (which happened to be in the direction they were going) the ground soon began gaining elevation with you barely noticing.

Normally, Erina went around. It was flatter, but further. Today was all about short-cuts. It wasn't the path you wanted to take when carrying a heavy load (or a fragile one) or even when you wanted to conserve energy and didn't have to worry about stopping for the night.

Today she didn't need to worry about any of that. The first thing she needed to do was to get back to where she'd left the tracks yesterday. She could re-evaluate after that. As such, she pushed Hollow to go faster.

The forest itself stretched on far around and above. Had she'd been able

* Which was murder when it came to the wind … it just never stopped.

to see it through the now thick cover of tree branches over her head, she'd see them hugging the mountain just as closely uphill, after having turned into little more than different types of pine trees on the higher elevations. There it would eventually give way to ice and snow as the taller mountains behind those rose, and rose, and rose. And those were still only the vanguards to Snowfell.

She didn't need to see them to know they were there.

There was green hugging the bases still. Hollow patches in dips and trenches away from the wind and cold. Snowfell itself, from a distance, looked to be nothing more than a barren, icy, waste hidden under thick layers of snow.

There was a larger glacier up somewhere that way, too, if Erina's memory served. She'd caught the briefest of glimpses when she'd first arrived in the Valley. A *very* brief glimpse. She'd been a bit preoccupied with *not dying* at the time to pay any real attention.

As such, it was a warm, and sweaty, pair that finally caught up with the trail Sam and Wave Rock had left behind.

'Judging by the direction, it looks like he's heading up,' Erina muttered. 'What the blast is he thinking?'

The two of them took a tiny detour when catching the sound of a tiny, trickling, stream. Taking the opportunity to stop to rest and fill up on their water, Erina was soon back in the saddle.

'Watch where you're going, Hollow,' she mumbled as she steered them up a barely visible game trail. 'The mountain side is more unpredictable than you think.'

By this time she wasn't actively looking for traces of her missing companions, more scanning ahead to guesstimate what direction they were likely taking and what their goal might be.

She'd been up this way before, though not often. It was many days ride from the stable under normal circumstances — though the actual distance wasn't *that* great. The terrain just kept you from being able to go fast anywhere. And where you did go, you were exhausted when you got there.

It would have gone faster if she'd known just how hard she could push the black stallion. But, while he'd improved exponentially since first arriving, he was a long way from having the stamina Harlan did.

As such, they took frequent breaks despite the feeling of urgency growing when, still, there was no sign of Sam or Wave Rock.

'It here where a couple of wings would really, really have helped,' Erina grumbled.

Hollow treated every new step with suspicion. Erina might have been here before but he hadn't. He'd never been this far away from home, any home, before. Fear was always the second emotion lurking behind every other thought in his mind.

Whatever they were heading to, he hoped they were getting closer. He was getting tired. His nerve ends were tingling. Hair was standing in places where hair really shouldn't be.

Though distance in the Valley was ambiguous at best, and an outright lie on occasion, Erina had learnt that there was (usually) a maximum afforded space the distance was allowed to take up.

Getting there might take an hour or a day or anything in between, but that predetermined boundary remained fixed from a set point. The same distance between two other points didn't. Sometimes it, to her, made no sense.

If it took longer than the highest estimate, another reason — like getting turned around — was more likely to be the culprit. Or going in circles. She'd done that a fair few times, especially early on. One tree looked much the same as another to someone who'd spent a large part of their life in space.

Simply getting stuck in stubbornly unshifting brambles or having to take the long way around to avoid sinkhole prone territory was just another day in your life here. Erina grimaced as she leaned forward in the saddle as they climbed up a particularly steep incline to save time.

Once at the top, Hollow breathing heavily, they stopped again. Both to rest and to re-orient themselves. That is, Erina did. Hollow was just grateful for the break.

Trying to look at the map she had in one hand, have another eye on their surroundings, another on the wildlife, and a last one on her mount was not easy.

For starters, she was coming up several sets of eyes short.

The paper-plastic combo sheet threatened to tear out of her grip, slapping her in the face. Swearing at it, it was unceremoniously stuffed into a pocket.

It was amazing how much you could fit into the pockets of this new coat of hers. It was really handy at keeping the wind out, too.

The two climbed ever upwards like small moving shadow ants on a, surprisingly forested, anthill. No longer unsure about his own legs, the black and red stallion's hooves clipped and clopped against the increasingly rocky ascent.

Erina was leaning forwards in the saddle, feet straining against the stirrups, letting Hollow pick his own path. It wasn't the first time she was up here, but it *was* Hollow's.

And, to be honest, having been here before didn't make the landscape easier to traverse.

In the early evening, they settled down at camp — which in this case was a bedroll and some collected twigs set alight and protected by scavenged stone. A bit bare bones for Erina, but with far less complaints from Hollow.

Then, Hollow, who'd been standing placidly a little ways from the fire, apparently asleep, jolted into action as if struck by lightning.

'Hey! What *are* you doing?'

Erina's shout betrayed her surprise. She shot to her feet, fingers grabbing for her weapon and wondering what the blazers was going on.

Hollow, coated in the darkness of the night, ran through the sudden stop/start again. And again.

Each time he'd more leap than run, then screech to a halt in a shower of small rocks and gravel and clods of dirt. It took Erina several more times, and a loud squeal, before she caught sight of the pelt of some sort of small animal, close to the ground. It dashed this way, then that, hiding beneath, or inside, anything it could.

Putting her hands on her hips, her lips quirked, Erina shook her head. As a hunter Hollow left a lot to be desired.

Even now, in good condition and well fed, he was mostly a jumble of legs and neck, running around trying to bite but ending up with nothing but air between his fangs.

After a few minutes, sides heaving, Hollow returned. The horse looked dejected.

'Got away did it?' Erina asked, chuckling. 'Somehow, I'm not surprised.'

She patted him affectionately on the neck, rubbing his forehead — careful to avoid cutting herself on any of the horns.

'Alright, alright, oh mighty hunter. Shall I, the master of scritches and overlord of the realm of supplies deign to catch you a tasty treat?' she asked.

A good thing she'd packed plenty of dehydrated meats. For this occasion, however, a nice bit of dried jerky proved even more welcome. She split the piece in two, helping herself to one and holding out the other to Hollow. He snapped it up with sharp teeth.

As their search continued, it became less a search and more of a question of how long it'd take to get to their goal. Erina had gotten a good idea about where Sam had gone at this point. This also meant she grew more irritated with having to go all this way and less worried about him.

On a more positive note, both horse and rider grew more and more in sync. They hadn't spent this much time alone together since Hollow first arrived at the stables and while the stallion remained jittery in comparison to some he was learning to trust his two-legged companion's judgement.

Well, mostly. Certainly not enough to trot over a floating stone bridge across a lake of boiling lava or anything similar. Thankfully, the Valley didn't have any. Not any that Erina had come across, at least.

'If Sam's gone where I think he has, we're close,' Erina mumbled. She looked up at Hollow. 'Think you can keep going just a little longer? If we go slow at night we should get there by morning.'

A little later and the black stallion picked his way forward through a terrain that was slowly levelling out, no trace of his usual hesitation.

'It's very handy that you can see in the dark. Which is more than can be said for me,' Erina said, waving her hand in front of her face.

Erina felt that the sound of Hollow's hoof beats in the night were alert, even strange, compared to the exact same sound during the day.

Except it *wasn't* the same sound. It never was. No matter how familiar, at night, everything sounded different. It was … comforting … Erina thought. It kept the world far away, which was just where she liked it to be.

One of the many reasons she'd always liked space. Sure, it was dangerous, but most of the time your interaction with other people was conducted with both an empty distance *and* several metal walls between you and them.

The reason for the dark was easy to trace. And it wasn't just because of the trees — up here they were sparse and less a forest than a moor with the occasional trunk that just hadn't given up. There was little light to be had from the sky.

It was unusual not to see at least one moon up. When you had four, you always seemed to have at least one spare.

The thing was, they probably were up. But the thin slivers of waning crescents were hidden behind a very thick layer of clouds that had sneakily rolled in during the late afternoon.

They'd been threating to rain on her the entire day. They didn't just block the moons, either. They blocked the space stations, too. And the stars.

Of them all, Erina was definitely more upset about the stars. She liked stars. They always reminded her that there was a wider world out there. More wonder. More adventure. More freedom.

'At least my hairs aren't tingling,' Erina mused. The tingle in her body that suggested a thunderstorm was promising it'd come around any day now was an excellent meter of deciding when to keep your head down and put your feet up in front of the fire. 'Good. We don't need this place to go all slippery on us. Bloody Seranthiem. Couldn't you have told me if you were going off and disappearing on us?'

Hollow stopped for a moment, deciding which way to go around a particularly large boulder. Several stories high, it divided the space in front of them into two paths. Erina nudged him to the left.

'Suppose that defeats the purpose,' she sighed. Running a hand through her hair, Erina continued muttering to herself as, through the night, they went without sleep, instead continuing onwards.

Why was she going in this direction anyway? Had she established that? She couldn't remember. Every time she tried to think of a possible reason her mind felt all foggy.

As it turned out, whatever had set her on this path, it proved to be the right one.

'Well, isn't this quite the sight,' Erina grumbled, her bleary eyes growing just a little bit larger than usual when, as dawn had broken and gone, the dark duo finally stumbled upon their quarry. 'Not the one I expected, either. I knew you were good with animals, Seranthiem. I didn't know you were *this* good.'

Despite the casualness of her words, Erina actually breathed a sigh of relief. She'd been more worried than she cared to let on.

'At least you're not hurt. Damn it, Sam. You scared me!' She scolded him from afar, though the last bit she muttered under her breath, just in case he could hear her even over this distance.

They'd made their way into the small, sunken, vale through the rocky opening, to find a veritable, verdant, paradise. In truth, the sight was a serene montage she'd normally have been loath to disturb.

Seranthiem was sitting beneath a leafy, green, tree with a thick brown trunk where, even from this distance, Erina could see the ribbed layers of the bark. The partly visible roots, half of them led over the river bank of a trickling stream no thicker than you could step from one side to the other, but which had dug itself down through the soft loam that she could tell it was there more by the sound than by vision — it could just as well have been a very narrow ditch.

In fact, she might have missed it entirely if it wasn't for the small, barely a meter tall, waterfall where the stream cascaded over (though that made it sound like it had more energy than it did) a little further up, closer to the embankment on that side.

It collected in a shallow, clear, pond, after which it disappeared in white froth over the edge of the mountain.

There were several other trees of the same sort dotted along the stream, many of them slightly smaller. They looked, if anything, like a cross between an oak and a weeping willow, if such a thing was possible.

The entire world here smelled fresh, like early morning in the woods by the sea.

There were a number of rabbits, and things that looked enough like rabbits for her to still call them that, about. Most of them were happily munching on the grass out in the open glade, but a couple had snuggled up against Sam's side.

There were only a couple because a lot of the space had already been occupied by at least three squirrels, two pheasants that could have doubled as a rainbow, a hedgehog with prickly leaves instead of spikes, a small pile of hyraxes, what *might* have been a quokka, and a small Stromberg deer who had laid down on the other side.

There was also some sort of small songbird sitting on top of his head. Its light trill would answer its brethren in the trees and bushes. There were a lot more of them than there were of any other animal here. They were brightly coloured and flittered about, always just out of sight.

'This explains a lot,' Erina mumbled to herself. What exactly it explained she wasn't sure of. But it had to be something. It felt … significant … for some reason. As if something had been missing but was so no longer.

Most of what she did with animals like these were scare them off, even when she didn't mean to. She sighed at the thought. It was the deep sigh of someone who had long since accepted their fate of being — for some unknown reason — intimidating while sitting quietly on a chair on the far side of the room in a lounge the size of an entire shipport.

This time, however, the animals had a much faster, and more visceral, reaction to Hollow appearing in the entrance of their sanctuary. Some even hissed and arched their backs before scattering.

There was one who was pleased to see them. A soft neigh came from a little way's away. Not far off from where they'd entered the small, sunken in, depression between two parts of smooth mountain sides, Wave Rock stood out against the otherwise green background. He'd been calmly grazing together with a young stag, his horns little more than bumps.

Hollow didn't acknowledge him. His attention was elsewhere.

Erina glanced down, sensing the tension running through her mount at the sight of so many small, furry, critters scampering for the safety of burrows, trees, and, in one case, diving into the waterfall, swimming upwards, and disappearing over the edge.

The black stallion shifted, hooves stomping, as if ready to leap forwards — completely forgetting about the rider on his back.

'No, Hollow! These are *not* food!'

Erina struggled with the reins, trying to hold back the powerful predator beneath her with words and legs. Hollow might not be a *good* hunter, but he still was one. The creatures here knew that. He knew that. She knew that.

That didn't mean it hadn't momentarily slipped her mind.

One furry little thing stopped just long enough to chitter accusingly at the approaching pair then dashed off. Hollow snapped his jaws at it.

It didn't look like they'd taken Seranthiem by surprise as he was already looking right at them. Of course he was. He must have heard them even before he saw them. It wasn't like riding a horse through the underbrush was a quiet endeavour. Nor did Hollow possess the elegance of a panther stalking his prey.

One thing Erina was certain of. This was clearly not the first time any of the now scattering menagerie had been here.

Just how that could be she had no idea. It was certainly the first time he'd been absent from the stable for any serious length of time. It wasn't like it had taken only a few hours to get here.

Unless he'd found a short-cut. Her eyes narrowed. Had he?

'Seranthiem.' Erina gave her errant lost soul a curt nod, then nudged Hollow forward while tightening the reins even further. It wouldn't do to have him suddenly decide that he was a mighty hunter after all.

Sam stood up as the two shadows clad in black and red approached. He gently lifted down the small bird from his head. It took off to land on a suitable branch nearby throwing them all as a dirty look as a bird was capable of.

There was a flurry of activity as multiple small feet decided they were better served by being elsewhere.

Not too far away, mind. Just enough that any lunging great beasts couldn't get them in a single leap. Some of them scampered up the walls, leaping and climbing on tiny irregularities in the rock's surface.

All of them, however, complained.

'I trust your time is not too preoccupied?' Erina asked, quirking an eyebrow at him.

Sam didn't immediately reply, seeming to mull the idea over.

Erina flung one leg over the neck in-front of her saddle and semi leapt down to the ground. She kept one hand on to the reins … just in case.

There had been a lot of small, furry, critters here just a moment ago. Now that there weren't, Hollow didn't seem interested in chasing after any of them anymore. How peculiar, Erina thought, before turning her attention to her errant companion.

'Thought you'd be back by now,' she said, giving him one of "those" looks.

Seranthiem, who'd been surprised to see her, wasn't sure why she looked so upset with him. Had he done something wrong? He did get days off … technically. It wasn't like there was anywhere to go. Okay, there were a lot of places to go but only as long as you remained inside the Valley. But the point still stood.

'What kind of greeting is that?' he asked, getting to his feet and straightening his clothes.

'The kind you get when you go *disappearing*!'

'Something came up.'

'You could have told me.'

'I left a note?'

That last counter volley stumped Erina. Such a simple question, yet such a nuisance to answer, literally. Communication — distant communication — that wasn't covered by shouting louder, wasn't just difficult at High Fyelds. It simply wasn't.

'What note?' Erina asked.

Seranthiem held back a deep sigh. This was precisely the reason why he *had* left a note in the first place. To avoid situations just like this.

'I left a note on the table, under the water jug,' Sam said. 'One of those bright orange stickers you're so fond of. Very visible.'

Erina racked her brain. Had there been one? She couldn't recall seeing one and she'd be willing to swear she'd looked everywhere for him. An obvious note like that should have been among the first things she'd have spotted.

Admittedly, she'd been looking for a person, not a piece of paper.

'I don't suppose it's too much to ask for that you're secretly a telepath or something like that?' Erina asked. 'For future escapades I mean.'

'You've watched too many holos.' Sam simply shook his head, taking in the exhausted looking person before him. He'd never meant for anyone to worry on his behalf. 'If I had been, I would have informed you of my delay,' he said.

‘I don’t know,’ Erina drawled sarcastically. ‘Would you have?’

‘Of course, My Lady.’

‘Riiight…’

If Erina’s tone hadn’t already betrayed the fact that she didn’t believe him, the eye-roll certainly did.

Crossing her arms, she plopped onto the ground with a heavy thud. ‘Fine,’ she muttered. ‘I’ve got no clue to what’s going on, but we’re going right back home first thing tomorrow.’

‘Of course, My Lady,’ Seranthiem said. He continued to apologise. What else could he do?

‘I didn’t mean to lose track of time.’

‘How long have you been here for?’ Erina asked.

‘As I left High Fyelds yesterday morning, about a day.’

‘WHAT?’

FOOD FOR THOUGHT

Once finding Sam, returning to High Fyelds proved undramatic. For Darklight Valley one might even say anticlimactic.

Harlan would have called the journey back boring, except he wasn't there to complain. Erina had to admit that riding Hollow — as long as he didn't spook — made for a much less jittery and calmer experience.

She hadn't been paying attention on the way out, but on the return journey, the change of the seasons really began to show themselves in all sorts of tiny little ways.

Though autumn was beginning to nip on the heels of summer, it made itself more remembered in the preparations for the season around the stable than in the weather itself.

Sam had listened, calmly, to how they usually prepared for winter and had, right then and there, decided that nope, that's certainly not what they were doing this year. He was not enduring being partially, or wholly, snowed in *and* having that little variety in his diet.

There was no reason to. The whole Valley was full of edibles that, if you prepared them right, had no trouble lasting years in a proper root cellar. It'd certainly last through winter, assuming you didn't eat all of it.

Though Erina had said that, before then, they'd need to make at least one trip to the outside world for everything they talked about wanting, though this was mostly not food related. Not anymore.

Still, there was something to be said about making your own.

As such, a host of ripening fruit and vegetables would soon stock the larder with jams and preserves from floor to ceiling. Salted meats were Erina's favourite but, when he suggested they'd make their own sausages, she put her foot down.

Mostly it was the plant side of the food wheel that they needed extra of. It wasn't as if the fish, fowl, or other critters, could migrate over winter in the Valley — though some did move between the different areas.

'Just *how* did you get in there?' Erina asked one afternoon as she, noticing one of the doors slamming, ever so regularly, against the wall stuck her head into one of the larders and ended up having to shoo an enterprising group of hyraxes of it before they decimated the dry-cured hams.

With all the extra, and new, items that Sam was planning to add to their stock-pile for winter, the normal larder in the house just wasn't big enough. Refurbishing one of the attachments to the main house, however, came with drawbacks.

Uninvited guests included.

Maybe she should look into how to build something to smoke some of it? Smoked fish were especially tasty.

She'd barely walked around the corner before the loud noise of wood slamming on wood, came back. This time the culprit was just a little bit bigger.

'Hollow! What are you doing?' she exclaimed as soon as she stepped through the door, after propping it open.

Having found a pitch black and red body more or less squashed into far end of the new storage room she narrowed her eyes.

'Out!' Erina ordered, pointing towards the door.

Hollow paid no attention. If anything, he tried to squeeze himself even further into the deepest, darkest, corner.

His ears were pricked forward. His largest horn dug furrows into the wall. Eyes aglow with intensity, the horse was super focused.

His object of attention; the far corner. Or, more accurately, the *bottom* far corner.

As Erina's eyes adjusted to the dim lighting in here the reason became obvious.

'Ah, rats!' Erina exclaimed. 'Oh well, I suppose it's a small blessing you didn't get into the living room or the kitchen.'

'Indeed,' Sam agreed, having come over to hear what all the fuss was about. 'There is still no door and it's a deep drop into the … basement. Not sure how we'd get him out if that happened.'

'In pieces, possibly.'

'My Lady!'

'That was a joke. By the seven stars of Solon, lighten up a bit Sam. Oh, and we should probably do something about that,' Erina pointed at the corner.

'Yes, *we* should,' Sam agreed.

For someone so decisive once she'd made up her mind about something, it was remarkable how long it could take her to actually make it, Sam thought. Not unlike a first generation QDE drive, her boot-up sequence and initial inertia was high, and then some, but once everything was in motion there was little you could do to stop it.

Running it straight into the wall wouldn't result in a sudden stop. It would only mean there was no more wall.

'Harlan never caused all this trouble,' Erina complained … conveniently forgetting that the inquisitive trias stallion had been causing all different ones.

'You get Hollow,' Sam said, throwing her a halter he'd grabbed from next door. 'I'll see if I can find out more about the rats. And hold on to him, please. I don't need five sets of stab wounds in my back.'

As it turned out, one of those things proved a lot easier than the other.

Sam glanced over to where the other horses were. Harlan appeared to be asleep. The only thing he could see were his hindquarters. The rest of him was turned away.

Wave Rock, on the other hand, though standing in the same spot, had his ears pricked forward, intent on the sounds from their people, trying to figure out if they were meant for him.

'Go figure,' Erina muttered as she eventually managed to get Hollow out of the room. 'Always asleep when you need him.' She turned to the black horse, shifting her attention to him. 'And don't go sneaking in next door, either, you hear?' she said.

Unlikely as that was considering how tight she was holding on to the lead rope, it was the voice of someone who desperately hoped that their future wouldn't include having to chase him out … again. At this rate they'd need a sturdier door. And walls, she reminded herself. No way was she going to share their hard-earned food with rats.

'I'll close the door,' Sam said, shutting the one to the new storage room. 'Still more work to be done it seems.'

'It never ends, does it?'

'Not that I know of.'

Erina slipped the halter over Hollow's head and gave him some scritches near the bottom of his horns. He closed his eyes for a moment, then trotted away towards where his friends were.

'Wise choice Hollow. Good thing we don't have more horses, eh?' Erina said, leading to Sam turning his head sideways towards her. 'Can you imagine how many of these we would need?'

Erina waved her hands over the saddles, bridles etc that were taking up a miniscule amount of space in the tack room next door. The only reason there weren't just two (the number of horses they had*) was because there were a couple of different types … and a number of broken ones.

'Not necessarily,' Sam countered. Going back to polishing the bridle in his hands, the smell of the polish and the leather was filling the morning air.

'Huh?'

'Simply put,' he continued, 'more horses does not necessarily equal more equipment. Not unless you require a designated set for each horse.'

'Easier that way,' Erina said. 'Less fiddling around with fittings.'

'More maintenance,' Sam pointed out.

'Hmm, I'll have to defer to you on that.' Judging by her expression, Erina was having her doubts. 'Anyway, almost done with this lot. Let's finish these then go take care of our rat problem.'

By the time she put the final piece down, admiring the gleam on the newly polished leather, the thick scent in the air, she heard a nicker from outside.

Putting the saddle back on the rack, she stuck her head out through the door, holding on to it in case Hollow was around and wanted to get into this

* Used to have…

room, too.

It wasn't Hollow.

'How you' doing boy?' Erina asked the trias.

Harlan nickered in response and begged for treats.

Erina laughed. 'Calm down you big silly. I'll bring you a treat. Don't you go sticking your head in my pockets again, you hear? Polish don't taste good, I promise.'

'Treats aren't the only thing that comes in tins,' Sam said, allowing himself a small, amused, smile.'

'Exactly,' Erina patted Harlan on the muzzle. 'Don't you go fussing. You'll get an once-over and polish, too.'

That was another thing that was on the day's to-do list, though she decided to wait for Sam to finish up as well before moving on to that task. It had been fine going back and forth between things when it had just been her and Harlan, but when, suddenly, there were three horses it took a bit more planning.

Thankfully, there was plenty of time left in the day and, soon enough, they could move on to the next chore. It still involved polish, after a fashion, but unlike the tack, the recipients were a lot more likely to try and move about.

Sam nudged Harlan and, a click at the back of his throat later, the horse lifted his left back hoof so that he was able to inspect it. It looked to be in good condition, so Sam rubbed on some of the special healthy-hooves oil that they'd picked up from the storage area.

One of Erina's many acquisitions during her previous outing no doubt, Sam thought. They were running low on that, too, it seemed. Another thing to add to the ever growing list supply list. He wondered how in the world she planned on carrying everything back.

For that matter, how had she managed until now? There was a lot at the stables that certainly hadn't been made here. Most things, actually. With only one horse, and without being able to order a cargo ship to drop everything off, how long had it taken to shift everything? Or was there something he wasn't seeing here?

Anyway, the product was good, there was no doubt of that. It was going the extra mile, so to speak, in keeping the hooves nice, shiny, and strong. He knew the brand, though it wasn't one his previous employers had favoured.

But then, unlike their horses, or Wave Rock for that matter, Harlan wasn't shooed. It wasn't as if there was a local blacksmith hiding away in a cave somewhere.

'Everything seems good,' Sam said straightening up. He gave Wave a solid couple of pats on the muscular rump. 'They could do with getting their manes and tails trimmed a bit. Especially Hollow. Any longer and we'll have to start tying it up.'

Erina felt that was a bit of an over-exaggeration. The black and red strands had grown considerably these last few months. Naturally wavy, it gave him a very particular look.

'Maybe we should have cut it a bit shorter the first time,' she mused.

'Perhaps.'

They watched the three horses wander over to check if there was still some feed left and, when there turned out to be none, head over to the edge of the closest field.

'And stay away from the vegetables, you hear!' Erina shouted after them.

'Since we're not likely to restrict the horses to the paddock, perhaps we should put a fence around the garden instead?' Seranthiem suggested.

'You're right. We should. Yet another thing to add to the to-do list,' Erina yawned and stretched her arms over her head, cracking her neck. 'We'll have to find the time for that, too, I suppose.'

'The stable could do with more life, ah, I mean help, around here,' Sam said. 'Perhaps there would be less work if there were more people?'

Erina looked positively aghast at the suggestion. One person extra was about all she could handle, voluntarily.

'I think not,' she replied. Taking the humans out of the equation, she considered the idea further. 'We could always get a cat. A pet one, I mean. Might actually be good around the stable.'

Sam chuckled lightly at the idea. 'I thought we already had one,' he said.

'Have what?'

Sam nodded towards the black and red stallion now prancing around out in the nearby field. At least it looked like he was prancing. It might have been meant to be more like a fox leaping onto some tiny prey. One that kept getting away.

‘A cat, I mean,’ Sam said.

Erina tilted her head to the side. ‘I don’t know… You’d think he’d be gifted with a little more grace if he had been.’

Once the horses had been fed and groomed, the two of them retired to the main house.

That is, Erina vanished into what was slowly becoming an office-library-unfinished-stuffs room as the living room was still under repair, while Sam rolled up his sleeves in the kitchen.

It was important to have time, lots of time, when they weren’t under each other’s feet. Most of those times, however, came in shorter increments. Normally it wasn’t an option to stay out of each other’s way for days on end*.

Unlike Erina, who either chose to spend hers holed up or out riding, Sam could often be either found in the kitchen, in the fields nearby, or reading his way through the small library.

‘A good thing I prepared this earlier,’ he mumbled to himself as he took the now ready dough out of the cooling pantry, lifting the tartan kitchen towel to check on it.

The chores around the stable had taken longer than he’d expected. But, with this, now he just needed to finish the rest and pop the round, flat, treats into the oven.

He’d prepared that, too, in advance, checking in on it from time to time to make sure the fire was still calm and steady. It needed plenty of time to heat up, but once it was, the separate compartments meant you could do multiple things at a time.

They key to using it was *doing* multiple things at a time. It was a bit of a waste of heat — and firewood — otherwise. A wrinkle appeared around his mouth. He enjoyed working with it, but using it took a lot of planning. He really needed to convince Erina to get them one that was, well, more instant. The problem was they didn’t exactly run on fusion cores or something. Maybe they could hook it up to run on hydropower? Would that work? Question was how to get the power from the stream all the way into the kitchen. Maybe some sort of gas?

As Sam continued to ponder the idea, and the potential solutions, the

* Well, there was. It just wasn’t a very good one.

kitchen was soon filling up with the sounds and scents of cooking and baking mingling happily together.

The scent of baking was what finally enticed the only other person here out of their own little world. Soon enough Erina was wolfing down a baked scone dripping with butter and strawberry jam. Polishing that one off, she then looked around for a second serving … or, possibly, the promise of something even better.

'Easy there,' Seranthiem admonished her, between nibbling on his own scone. 'Eat *slower*. The food is not going anywhere, I swear it.'

This didn't have quite the result he'd expected and the food on the table was soon devoured down to the last crumbs.

'I suppose I should be grateful you didn't eat the table while you were at it,' Sam mumbled.

'What was that?'

'Nothing, My Lady.' Sam coughed discreetly. 'I was hoping to use some of the leftovers for the excursion tomorrow. I imagine you will not be hungry come dinnertime?'

'You should have said something,' Erina said. 'And why in the world wouldn't I be?'

Sam was sensible enough that, this time, he bit his tongue before he actually responded.

❊❊❊

Waking up early was never fun, as far as Erina was concerned. Sometimes, though, it was a necessary evil. It was a good thing they'd prepared the packs the night before. Doing so now wouldn't just be a giant time sink, she'd unerringly find out — come nightfall — that they contained, among other things, two dozen packets of raisins, a small foldable pickaxe, and the box with last night's leftovers … completely sans leftovers as they had been eaten at some point in the night.

She'd learnt long ago to do almost everything but actually waking up the night before. And if it had been an option to do that too, she would have.

As it was, the cool morning air hit her in the face. Cantering along the side of the fields, the brisk chill stung her skin, waking her up. The winds had been promising, and they didn't disappoint.

Erina pulled up sharply. Hollow applied the breaks, sliding a bit as he dug all four hooves into the still dewy grass.

Wave Rock, who'd been following at a more sedate pace, simply trotted on until he and Sam had caught up with the other pair.

'Harlan! No!' Erina called out as the trias looked to move ahead without them. It seemed, for a moment, as if he was going to anyway, then he snorted, tossed his head, and just stood there, a painted tricoloured picture against a blue and white sky.

Down below — one of the herds of wild horses* covered the gently sloping hill. None of the herds were terribly big, but there were several of them, spread out over the Valley.

Here, they surrounded a grey rock monument (if that's what it was) that towered above them. The only pieces of colour in this world of green.

'Is it some sort of Megalith?' Sam had asked the first time he'd seen it. Erina had shrugged. It could just be very weathered building blocks of what was left of a rock gazebo. Whatever it was, it was old. Neither of them needed an archaeologist to tell them that. It had to be dating back to when there had actually been inhabitants living here. Probably all the way back to when this valley hadn't even been a valley.

'Always impressive,' Sam said, giving the stones a nod. 'I do hope it doesn't intent to give us trouble in the future.'

In his experience, which, admittedly, wasn't that long, everything in the Valley did … sooner or later. It might not even mean to, as if somehow that made things better?

'Hopefully we won't find out it's an interdimensional energy conduit only accessible during a planetary convergence,' Erina quipped. She made a small huff at the idea. 'Not like we'd get any advance warning.'

'I don't think we'd need to worry about that,' Sam chuckled. 'Even if it *was* one, it's a bit too broken to actually function properly.'

'Maybe the broken bits are the unimportant ones? Who knows? Impressive lumps of stone, though. Glad I don't have to move them anywhere.'

* Not that the Valley contained a whole lot of tame critters.

Overall, there weren't a lot of structures in the Valley. At least not ones that she'd found — though considering how most of it was covered in trees and the rest might have been buried beneath windblown soil, rock-falls, or creeping ice, that didn't really mean anything.

Also, there was the tiny detail of finding the best preserved one of them all right under her bloody house. Probably best not to jump to any conclusions other than it was a strange place that she'd come to live in.

The odd thing was, it was also seemed a *tiny* bit bigger than when she'd first come here.

Back then most constructed thing she'd known of had been the crashed* shuttlecraft that she'd lived out of. It was still out there, in the same location it had come down in. It wasn't like she'd been able to move it.

True, it had been rather stripped down over the years and was more akin to a shell these days. It certainly wasn't going to be flying anywhere — unless hurled into the air by an unexpected geyser or something.

She'd left enough that it still made for a good shelter. It certainly was nicer than a mere campfire on the ground. It *might* also have seen some things *added* to it to make it more comfortable.

The crash. Erina made a wry face as the memories came flooding back. She reached out to pet the slender neck in front of her. It felt warm beneath her hand. It was a good way to stay grounded.

The memories, they were becoming more distant every year, and a good thing that was. There were other things she wished the years would diminish, but which were as clear, and emotional, as the time they'd come from. Some scars never truly healed. You merely forgot what it was like not to have them. Not that she'd ever had anything to compare with … there.

Also, that had *not* been one of her finer piloting moments despite that, in hindsight, it was nothing short of a miracle that the shuttle had come down *mostly* intact. What it should have done is rain little pieces of metal and boiled blood and ash all over the forest before finishing the breaking apart that had begun in the upper atmosphere and explode in a shower of fire.

Of course, according to conventional wisdom there shouldn't have been a forest there to begin with. Nor anything else. Who the blazers expected to run

* Which was still "built" in the technical sense even while in pieces, just not very useful.

into[*] a mountain, a forest, or anything else solid *here*? Between the stratosphere and the thermosphere you had clouds on one end and maybe the risk of running into an orbiting satellite on the other.

Oh, and occasionally other ships.

A bloody mountain had *not* been high on her list. Glancing upwards, the infernal thing still loomed in the distance. She went up there regularly. More out of sheer spite than any real need. As if needing to tell the mountain it had lost that fight.

Of course, up until she'd crashed on, or in, it, no one had actually known it was there at all. Until she got out of here the first time, they still hadn't. Quite the feat for something that large, Erina thought. One thing was certain, the geological feature didn't like to be noticed and was *probably* not entirely geological in nature in the first place. Not even Seranthiem could argue with her on that one, for all that he felt common sense dictated that he should.

She still hadn't found an answer to any of those questions. If anything, every year in the Valley just presented her with *more* questions, usually without having the curtesy of answering her earlier ones first.

Unless said answers just led to more questions.

'Vindictive, petty, little thing you are,' Erina would mutter at times when she felt especially haunted.

Of course, "normal" on a planet like Casticia had been a big old question mark even back in the old days. By now it had metamorphosed[†] and even the definition had changed, or, at the very least, been argued about.

If anything, the strange phenomenon that were so prevalent in the Valley had begun to show evidence of themselves in the rest of the world, too. Or, Erina corrected her train of thought, had begun to show up where enough people were being people so as to be able to notice them.

Maybe they had always been there? Maybe they *were* increasing? Who was to say? Casticia was, after all, mostly unexplored wilderness — and its people were keen on keeping it that way.

'Who knows what might be hiding out there?' Erina asked of the air. 'In the rest of the world, I mean. I'm just saying, if they see Cthulhu's second

[*] Quite literally…

[†] Quantum might have been involved somewhere … then told to go home from playschool.

cousin washing ashore after a storm I'm never going sailing again!'

'There have been extensive mapping and surveys done,' Sam argued. 'It's not like the Valley where almost everything is unknown.'

'Extensive closer to the settlements, yes,' Erina agreed. 'Head out beyond that and everything we know becomes generalized real quick. Satellites only do so much. And I don't even have those to help me.'

'Auto surveys *can* only do so much,' Sam nodded. 'But the DragonCorps are new and few in number, for all the detail in their work. The lack of communication while in the air between dragon and rider is an inconvenience, I'm sure.'

Erina scoffed, waving away the argument with a dismissive gesture.

'Easier to survey a planet that is barren rock. And considering what we've found on some of those, I'm not even sure about that!'

Sam was right, of course. The DragonCorps *were* new. So new, in fact, that she'd actually been around when it had first been created. They hadn't really had time to make their mark, as the expression went.

It would have been easier if she'd been able to invite them to map Darklight Valley. They didn't need to rely on machinery to stay in the air. Flying certainly had its advantages and, at times like these, she missed her ship.

Erina sighed. She was a lot of things, but a cartographer certainly wasn't one of them. Besides, the only time she'd seen it from above there had been clouds, a mountain, and a whole lot of *down* going on.

She did have a rudimentary idea of the closest main features, but the further towards the edges you were, or the more details you looked for, the less she was certain of, well, anything.

Needless to say, Sam had given up on trying to use the map she'd made of the Valley. It might make perfect sense to Erina, but to anyone else it was two squiggles away from being invited to a showing at an abstract art gallery.

Taking her eyes away from the wild horses, Erina focused on her companion. 'We can swing by the upside-down-stream on the way back if you'd like? You haven't seen that yet, have you?'

Sam made a noise suggesting that no, he hadn't'[*].

[*] He had.

A much louder, and far more insistent, noise came from Hollow, who was stomping his hooves on the ground impatiently.

'Fine. Fine. We're going,' Erina groused, swinging over from one horse to the other without touching the ground. 'I swear, you're so impatient sometimes. This time remember, the other horses are more scared of you than you are of them, so be nice.'

The red and black stallion danced excitedly beneath her, reins whipping with the motion. Harlan let out a displeased neigh, not happy he had to share this outing and *his* two-legs if they were going to go around making a fool of themselves.

'Toss me one of those peaches, why don't you, Sam?' Erina called out a little later when they stopped for a break.

'As you wish, My Lady,' Sam replied, making a small bow as he handed over the ripe fruit. It smelled warm and sweet even from a distance, though that might just be the fact they were currently camped out beneath the peach tree in question.

A loud harrumph erupted from Erina as she pinched her nose, practically squashing it between her fingers.

'How many times … *Seranthiem* … have I told you *not* to call me that?'

There was the barest twitch to the corner of her companion's mouth. A crack in the otherwise oh-so-stoic façade. It wasn't the first time his face reminded her of that of a porcelain doll: The fair complexion that on another person would have been called unhealthy. The serene elegant features. His long silver hair. It was only the life in the grey eyes that betrayed his status as a live human*. Well, that and moving about, she supposed.

He'd make a good elf, she'd decided way back when first meeting him at Epsilon Courts. So far he hadn't done anything to change her mind about that. Quite the contrary.

'This would be the first time,' Seranthiem said, a little confused, waiting for Erina's mind to catch up.

'Then … Stop. It.'

Sam didn't look like he intended to be very compliant — though he didn't

* The idea of a living "doll" was horrifying in her mind. Probably why they kept making holos about them.

seem to do it nearly as often these days anyway.

'The nature of this relationship of employer and employee, with special consideration to the locale and means of living, doing otherwise would be improper.'

'Sam,' Erina, sounding exhausted, pleaded. 'At least do it less? Please? You're giving me a headache.' Literally *and* metaphorically, though Erina didn't say that last bit out loud.

'As you wish, Madame.'

There was a slight, amused, twinkle to the grey eyes as Sam spoke.

Erina shuddered as every word imaginable raced across her imagination. 'No. Nope. Not doing that! Absolutely not,' she said.

Sam chuckled ever so slightly. 'Very well.'

'Thanks. And Sam?'

'Yes?'

'There's absolutely no reason to sound like the *Encyclopaedia Septem Stellae* every time your feathers are ruffled.'

There was nothing but silence for a moment. If because Sam was utterly stunned or because he was simply waiting for her to finish, was anyone's guess.

'I'll understand the point all the same.' Erina held up a finger for emphasis. 'I'm not going to judge you for not being perfect all the time, you know that. Or *should* know that, by now.'

The voice trailed off a bit towards the end, but even with that Sam closed his eyes for just a fraction longer than usual as he carefully considered the words.

Of course he knew that. But knowing and putting into practice were two very different kinds of beasts. Beasties, as Erina liked to call them.

'I will … try … to remember,' he said. He spoke slowly. Meticulously. Every word, every syllable, enunciated with utmost care.

'As good a promise as any, Erina replied.

Clearly pleased with what she saw as a not-so-small victory, she clapped her hands together. If it was to celebrate or because she'd just remembered something, Sam didn't know. She was just as much a mystery to him today as the day he'd first arrived in the Valley.

Erina grinned at him.

'Lets ride!'

The wind whipped in the three horses' manes. Tails streamed behind them like tongued banners of dark flames.

It rippled through the cloak Erina wore and should, by all intent, have ripped the hood right off her head. The large, loose, abundance of material should have been gripped by the wind like a sail and attempted to strangle the person wearing it.

It didn't.

Sam, like always, was happy he kept his hair up in a high ponytail. The silver strands trailed behind him like pale rays of moonlight.

There was nothing before them but open plains stretching as far as the eye could see. Mountains enveloped in a growing fog faded into the sky until, if you didn't know they were there, they could be mistaken for clouds on the horizon. The air, crisp as only the first days of autumn could be, filled their lungs.

All three horses were running so fast now that the ground was becoming a blur. Rather than slowing down — which would have been the safer option — Erina leaned forwards and urged Hollow to even greater speed.

The black stallion stretched out. Feeling the grass beneath his hooves, every stride lengthened as they raced across the fields trying to outrun each other, the wind, maybe even the stars themselves.

Chrono-order of the Seven of Stars books

If you'd like to read the books in the order they actually take place within their universe, this won't be the order in which they have been written *or* published (this include some short stories not mentioned on this list).

The good thing is, you don't need to read them in any particular order to enjoy them and aside from "Chronicles of Sun & Moon", they are all able to be read as "stand-alones" even those *technically* in a "series".

The universe itself is divided into seven different **Ages**.

1st Age -3rd Age

4th Age

"The Damsel and the Dragon"

"Magical Mischief"

"You're a Dragon"

5th Age

"The Dawn of the Winds"

"Wolf's Bane"

Chronicles of Sun & Moon: Book 1: "Lord of the Wind"

Chronicles of Sun & Moon: Book 2 "Moontouched"

Chronicles of Sun & Moon: Book 3 "Island of Illusion"

6th Age

"The Soul Within"

"High Fyelds – A New Beginning"

"High Fyelds – The Big Race"

"High Fyelds – The Black Stallion"

7th Age

"Academia Draconia"

"Silberwing"

Also by Mae McKinnon

A world of Magic, Mystery, and Adventure

also Found Families, Sarcasm

& quite often Dragons

ACADEMIA DRACONIA

Gaile Ashworthey isn't cool. She isn't confident.
She certainly isn't brave.

Struggling with being a student at the prestigious Dragon Research Centre on New Retmia, Gaile feels like she'll never be able to graduate and become a dragonrider.

Then a mischievous dragonling stumbles into her life...

THE ACADEMIA DRACONIA SERIES:

ACADEMIA DRACONIA

SILBERWING

High Fyelds

Crashing into a mesa that doesn't exist, to survive, Erina quickly needs to learn that science isn't the only thing governing the Castician solar system. In Darklight Valley, there is only one ruler: Magic ... well, that and its mysterious guardian.

THE HIGH FYELDS SERIES:

HIGH FYELDS: A NEW BEGINNING

HIGH FYELDS: THE BIG RACE

HIGH FYELDS: THE BLACK STALLION

The Damsel and the Dragon

An isolated mansion populated, mostly, by ancient spellcasters lost in their own research and overseen by a famous Archmage doesn't seem the most likely place to meet your soulmate.

Setharrion is running away from an overbearing mother.

Linandra is running away from an arranged marriage.

It could be a match made in heaven, assuming she doesn't brain him with a frying pan for being a twat first.

THE SOUL WITHIN

Earth: Early 21st Century

After the alien invasion, most of the world lies in ruin. Their only hope now; a project scrapped years ago: five experimental F.U.R.I.

The Furies were meant to be piloted by the best humanity had to offer. When one of them selects thirteen year old Jo Wright instead, everything appears lost.

YOU'RE A DRAGON

GAMEBOOK

Get swept away into the world of Casticia in the Fourth Age. Will it be a time to enjoy the sights? Meeting old and new friends? Visit the temple city's famous bakeries?

Or, will you, perhaps, focus on figuring out how to deal with that, somehow, between here and there, you got turned into a dragon and if the spell isn't stabilized you will ... explode?

The choice is all yours!

Chronicles of Sun & Moon

Dive into a fantasy world being slowly brought to its knees, where a squabbling group of not-exactly-heroes-and-certainly-not-friends are dragged into a quest out in the monster-infested wilds.
This goes about as well as expected...
And as if battling ichor-dripping monstrosities intent on eating them alive wasn't enough, sometimes the real difficulty is facing yourself — or, in the case of Sun & Tal, each other.

THE CHRONICLES OF SUN & MOON TRILOGY:

LORD OF THE WIND

MOONTOUCHED

ISLAND OF ILLUSION)

Author's Note

Time. Time is something we all have (whether we want to or not apparently) but for me it seems like it's constantly slipping through my fingers – or it's taking a short-cut through some undiscovered wormhole which is why I keep ending up later in the day, week, month, or year than I thought I was*.
"Intense" they said this year was going to be.
This feels, in hindsight, as something of an understatement…

* Which is *very* annoying.

www.ingramcontent.com/pod-product-compliance
Lightning Source LLC
Chambersburg PA
CBHW021213160726
47994CB00001B/458
9789918956241